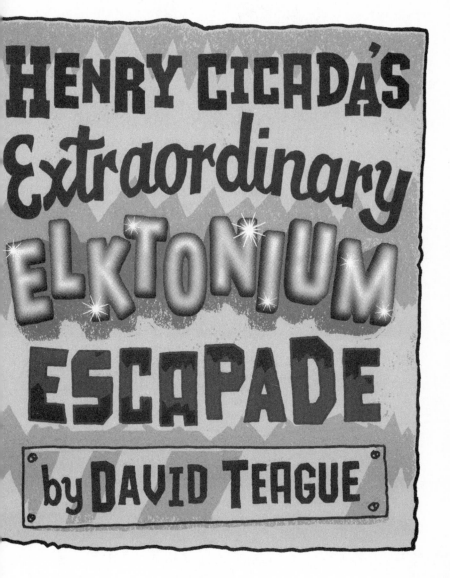

HENRY CICADA'S Extraordinary ELKTONIUM ESCAPADE

by DAVID TEAGUE

HARPER

An Imprint of HarperCollinsPublishers

For Warfield Teague,

who loves science as much as he loves storytelling

Henry Cicada's Extraordinary Elktonium Escapade

Copyright © 2016 by David Teague

All rights reserved. Printed in the United States of America.

No part of this book may be used or reproduced in any manner whatsoever without written permission except in the case of brief quotations embodied in critical articles and reviews. For information address HarperCollins Children's Books, a division of HarperCollins Publishers, 195 Broadway, New York, NY 10007.

www.harpercollinschildrens.com

Library of Congress Cataloging-in-Publication Data

Teague, David.

Henry Cicada's extraordinary Elktonium escapade / David Teague. — First edition.

    pages   cm

Summary: "Henry Cicada just wants to be plain, but extraordinary things keep happening to him. When he's accidentally transported to a different dimension, he realizes a little wackiness is the key to adventure"— Provided by publisher.

ISBN 978-0-06-237745-6 (hardback)

[1. Space and time—Fiction.   2. Adventure and adventurers—Fiction.   3. Science fiction.]   I. Title.

PZ7.T219375He 2016   2015009965

[Fic]—dc23   CIP

                                                          AC

Typography by Ellice M. Lee

15 16 17 18 19 PC/RRDH 10 9 8 7 6 5 4 3 2 1

❖

First Edition

A Plain Boy, Ideally

There was one thing Henry Cicada wanted more than anything else in the world. More than he wanted to change history with an outrageously brilliant scientific discovery (which his mother, Melissa, had come pretty close to doing, sort of, according to some people). More than he wanted to save a school bus full of children from plunging into a lake, more than he wanted to rescue courageous explorers trapped amid unknown dimensions of space and time, more than he wanted to defend the president from kidnappers and become a hero, yes, a *hero*, with freeways named after him.

What Henry wanted more than any of that, at precisely 8:00 a.m. on the first Tuesday after Labor Day, was to turn the knob on the front door of his house and sneak out to launch a quest for something of truly monumental importance: He wanted to be ordinary. Innocuous. Inconspicuous. Just plain *plain*.

Time for Henry to be going.

But first, he checked over his shoulder.

For you see, if Henry's dad caught him before he cleared out of 339 Bill Street for the day, ordinariness was not what he'd achieve. It'd be the opposite: notoriety. And burdened by notoriety, Henry would never fulfill his dream, which was to become an entirely new person, a plain one, so plain that he'd never stick out, never attract attention, never do anything remarkable or noteworthy ever again.

So intent on his quest was Henry that he stumbled over a small mound of his father's discarded, outmoded, obsolete, derelict, and downright ill-advised inventions, which scattered with a dull racket. *Yikes!* Had his dad heard?

Useless devices like these, every one made of Elktonium, an extremely rare and strangely glimmering metal, were stowed all over the house. They lurked in the closets, the spare shower, the garage, the attic, you name it. Now they had overflowed into the hall. Henry and his dad tripped over the contraptions all day long, and dodged them as they plunged off high shelves, and never once considered taking them to the dump, where they belonged.

As the clatter of falling Elktonium died away, Henry cringed, really, really hoping his dad had already gotten busy working in the basement and become, as usual, totally oblivious to everything else. He waited. He listened. The sound of faintly humming machinery emanated from beneath the floorboards. Nothing more.

Henry pushed the front door open six inches, holding his breath as it groaned, and he eased into the yard, lugging his book bag by the straps. Birds sang. The sun shone. A fresh breeze blew. Henry checked over his shoulder one last time. All clear. He'd made it! Heaving a sigh of relief, Henry turned to greet the brand-new day. And ran smack into his father's navel. Henry's dad was six foot five. "Henry!" said Henry's father, whose name was Phil. "I made a present for you! Out of Elktonium! To celebrate the first day at your new school!"

"Oh," said Henry to himself, "no."

But Phil had brought up an excellent point: it *was* the first day at Henry's new school. So if he intended to achieve glorious ordinariness, avoid notoriety, attain the dream, and all that, this was basically his only chance. Which was why he'd wanted to get out of the house undetected. Because the last thing Henry wanted to drag to sixth grade was another of his father's crackpot Elktonium gadgets, something he'd inevitably have to unveil at lunch, like his Elktonium lunch box; uncrate in the band room, like his Elktonium trumpet; use to calculate the hypotenuse in geometry, like his Elktonium triangulator; wear on his nose, like his Elktonium eyeglasses; or otherwise deploy embarrassingly.

Henry said, "Oh. Dad. Well . . ." He didn't want to hurt his father's feelings. But he *was* on a quest. To be plain. So he had to say it. "Maybe I could have my present *after* school?"

Completely ignoring Henry's suggestion and what it implied (namely, that Henry wasn't exactly crazy about his presents), Henry's father shouted, "Shoes!" whereupon he produced the aforementioned articles from behind his back. Henry had never seen such ugly footgear in his life. "I made them myself, by staying up late at night in the basement," said his father. He beamed at his monstrous creations, which kind of shimmered in the morning sunlight. "They're made of one hundred percent, highest quality, unadulterated—"

"Elktonium," said Henry glumly.

"Did I already mention that?" asked his dad.

"Yes," said Henry.

Now, in Henry's eyes, Elktonium was the emblem of every misfortune to have befallen him in his young life. Elktonium was the spring from which the trouble flowed. Elktonium, if you asked Henry, was the root of all evil.

Elktonium was a new metal, the first new metal in many years, an element on the periodic table down at the end where most scientists are scared to go. Henry's mother had ingeniously synthesized it and cleverly stabilized it to quash any pesky radioactivity and named it after her hometown: Elkton, Maryland. The fact was, Henry's mother *had* been something of a bold genius. She'd been Professor of Phenomenal Phenomenology at the prestigious Lookings Institute of Philadelphia, Pennsylvania, the most important scientific laboratory in the country. Unfortunately, because of Elktonium, Melissa's legacy as a brilliant scientist was now in decline, because apart from being the first new metal in many years, Elktonium had turned out to be pretty much worthless. It was three times heavier than lead, had an odd odor (kind of like tropical Mr. Clean), and was about as strong as heavy-duty Saran Wrap. It dissolved in lemonade, and dogs were slightly afraid of it. The one nice attribute of Elktonium was that it sometimes shimmered the same iridescent green as the lid of an old lady's pillbox. But that's not exactly useful, is it?

So what if Elktonium was a bust, was Henry's opinion. His mother had still been a great scientist, a great lady, and a great mom, and she'd worked hard every day on her last creation, Elktonium, even when she was so tired she could barely stand up in the lab. Why not leave it at that?

Because now the problem was, even though Elktonium had turned out to be basically no good to anybody, Henry's father, Phil, wouldn't admit it. He claimed that people just didn't *understand* Elktonium. He maintained that if Melissa had created it, then Elktonium must be good for something. The only problem was, no one had yet discovered what that something *was*. So Phil Cicada took it upon himself to uncover Elktonium's true purpose. He started inventing new devices made of Elktonium. The Elktonium Bootjack. The Elktonium Spatula. The Elktonium Wok. Phil began neglecting his job at the Free Library of Philadelphia, requests for old volumes of Walt Whitman's poetry began to pile up, and eventually Phil got himself fired. He and Henry had to move to Texas so Phil could operate the cash register in a 7-Eleven in a small desert town called Pumpjack, which, he told Henry, was the nearest location he could find employment, given his highly specialized work experience. Plus, Phil added, Texas was a spectacular place, with deserts, mountains, stars in the sky, and, some people claimed, on certain moonless nights, ghostly blue lights that traveled mysteriously to and fro in the distance. On the drive out from Philly, Phil had told Henry they should go look at the lights sometime, but so far they hadn't managed to get around to it.

Overall, Henry also got the idea his dad just wanted to get far away from Philadelphia, Pennsylvania, and the memories associated with it. And although the memories persisted, Phil had definitely succeeded in leaving Philly behind. Pumpjack was located just this side of Nowhere.

For the record, "Nowhere" is a point of reference Texans use because Texas is extremely large and easy to get lost in, as in the aforementioned "just this side of Nowhere." There is also "halfway to Nowhere," "the other side of Nowhere," "due south of Nowhere," and "not exactly Nowhere, but you can see it from there."

At the 7-Eleven, Phil's boss was seventeen years old, but very understanding about arranging a flexible work schedule, giving Phil plenty of spare time to take care of Henry as well as to tinker with Elktonium. Hence the shoes.

"The kids will certainly sit up and take notice of you in

these puppies!" Phil exclaimed, brandishing the extremely large, shiny shoes. For some reason, even though Henry was only five foot four, he had size fourteen-and-a-half feet, which made each Elktonium shoe about a foot and a half long.

A first-grader could almost use it for a canoe, thought Henry. *As long as he or she doesn't try to paddle it through a lake filled with lemonade, of course, which will dissolve it immediately.*

"I wanted your first day of school to be special!" continued Phil.

"I'm sure 'special' won't even *begin* to describe the kind of day I'm going to have, Dad," replied Henry, as all the things he *should* say to his father raced through his mind, things like, "There's no way in the world I'm wearing those shoes to school, because if I do, my dream of a brand-new, gloriously *un*-notorious start will go belly-up quicker than the class goldfish. These are the shoes Bigfoot would wear to the disco."

What Henry really said was, "They're, um, well—" He struggled to think of a word. "—*unprecedented*, Dad." Henry was pretty good at coming up with adjectives that *seemed* complimentary, even if, upon further inspection, maybe they weren't. Adjectives, for instance, like "unprecedented," which could mean something was so *great* there'd never been anything like it in history, or, on the other hand, could mean something was so *gosh-awful* there'd never been anything like it in history. This strategy kept Henry from having to lie to his dad all the time.

Henry's father handed him the glittering high-top moon-boot-like footwear he'd crafted secretly, late at night, out of love for Henry and a misguided desire to make the first day at his new school special. Henry closed his eyes and took a brief moment to silently bid his dream farewell: *Good-bye, dream.*

"Good-bye, Dad," said Henry out loud.

"Good-bye, son," said his dad.

Henry laced up his new shoes, put on his Philadelphia Phillies baseball cap, and headed for the bus stop.

First Name Jurgen,
Last Name Mintfarm

Henry trudged past his neighbor's house (the name on the mailbox read "General G. G. P. Hedgerow," but neither Henry nor his dad had ever met the man). He turned left at Sheila Street and made for the bus stop. Every twenty-three seconds, his Elktonium-rimmed glasses oozed down the bridge of his nose and had to be pushed back up, raising Henry's dork factor another notch each time.

Suddenly, a little golden-brown dog ran up carrying a bone, dropped it on the sidewalk, and showed his pointy teeth in what Henry figured was a smile, since the pooch was wagging his whole body in greeting (probably because his tail was so stubby that another good name for it would've been "nonexistent"). The puppy was missing his front right paw, but was also short one ear, which put him even again, since three paws plus one ear equals four.

The dog sniffed suspiciously at all the Elktonium associated with Henry and shivered. He backed up two steps, sat down, and, when he was a safe distance away, barked in a sociable tone. Henry knew making friends with a dog as far out of the ordinary as this one could put a kink in his quest for plainness, but he also felt pretty sure that bark would be the kindest sound he'd hear all day. So he took three seconds off his single-minded pursuit of plainness to pat the little guy's head. "What's your name, fella?" he asked. The dog shook its collar, and Henry noticed a tag on it that read "Pim Pom."

Henry didn't quite know what to do about the fact that Pim Pom was missing his front right paw. He wondered if he should say something about it, like, "Sorry about your leg, little fella," but since Pim Pom didn't act worried, Henry didn't worry, either.

"Wanna play fetch, Pim Pom?" Henry asked.

Pim Pom said, "Arf."

Henry picked up the bone and threw it down the sidewalk. Pim Pom looked at him funny and scuttled off to hide in a nearby bush, yelping hysterically. Unfortunately, the last time Pim had played fetch, it had ended terribly, though Henry had no way of knowing this.

"Gee whiz," Henry said sadly, gazing at the spot in the hedge where Pim Pom had disappeared. It seemed like Pim Pom had actually liked him there for a few seconds.

Henry shrugged and kept walking. He tried to tell himself it didn't matter. He tried to tell himself he didn't care. He tried to tell himself disappointment was no big deal. It happened to people all the time. After a few steps, Henry, who was staring off into space pretending nothing was the matter, tripped over Pim Pom's bone. He picked the bone up and put it in his lunch box, hoping maybe he'd run into old Pim later and have a chance to get their misunderstanding ironed out, even though Henry was also careful to tell himself it didn't matter much one way or the other, because, after all, ordinariness was his true objective, not making friends with little dogs.

Henry was the first person at the bus stop, so he sat on his trumpet case and waited. His new shoes, which emanated a pungent aroma of mango, coconut, and disinfectant, already felt like they were giving him a blister on the left heel. While he loosened his laces, a very small kid appeared, dragging a colossal trombone case behind him. The kid hunched over like he was afraid somebody might punch him in the belly any moment, and he glanced obsessively over his shoulder, as if he were a hunted fawn.

While Henry watched, this kid proceeded to set his trombone case on the ground, open it, climb in, and somehow lock it from the inside. Then he unlocked the case, stuck his head out, and said to Henry, "Knock three times when you see the bus."

"OK," said Henry. The kid disappeared back inside his horn case, which seemed to be made of fake alligator hide. Henry noticed several little holes drilled in one end to admit fresh air. At the other end was a label that read "Property of." Underneath "Property of" someone had written, in shaky green Sharpie, "Mintfarm, Jurgen."

"Say," Henry shouted into the air holes, "is that really your name? Mintfarm?"

"Yes!" hissed Mintfarm very loudly. "Go away!"

"Jurgen Mintfarm?" continued Henry.

"Yes!" hissed Jurgen Mintfarm.

"I'm Henry," said Henry. "Henry Cicada."

"Go away, Henry Cicada!" demanded Jurgen.

Well, Henry thought, looking at his ludicrous shoes, *I guess things could be worse. I could be four feet tall, stuffed in a fake-alligator-hide trombone case, and named "Mintfarm."* He figured that, all in all, it'd probably be better for everyone if he just dropped this conversation and set his sights back on ordinariness. But pretty soon, his curiosity got the better of him.

"Why are you hiding in your trombone case, Jurgen?" asked Henry.

Jurgen twitched like the worm in a jumping bean. "Shhh!" he hissed.

Fine, thought Henry. Actually, oppressive silence, now that he thought about it, could aid his quest to achieve plainness quite a bit. No talking, no outrageousness. So he sat and basked in the quiet.

For ten seconds. Then Henry saw what Jurgen was hiding from. Actually, *who* Jurgen was hiding from. A very large boy, very blond, very—well, "belligerent," "hostile," and "truculent" were words that came to mind. Plus, you could tell just by looking at him that this joker thought he was handsome, that he was the kind of kid to whom nearsighted school librarians, ditzy aunts, and drive-up-window cashiers would say, "Aren't you handsome?" And then, of course, he would have no choice but to agree, mostly because of the "charming" lock of blond hair that stuck up three-quarters of an inch from his forehead.

"Hey," said the allegedly handsome boy to Henry. "Isn't that, uh, Jurgen's trombone case?"

Henry shrugged. In his mind, he named this guy "Mr. Handsome."

"Listen," said Mr. Handsome, "don't get me started on those pathetic shoes you're wearing. Just tell me if you saw a little shrimpy scaredy-cat come by here."

Henry heaved a sigh, hoping to seem regretful because he couldn't answer this question, even though he wasn't regretful in the least.

Mr. Handsome said, "You're new. I know because I've never seen you here before, and now I see you." Henry couldn't argue with Mr. Handsome's logic (if "logic" was the name Mr. Handsome's thought process deserved), so he nodded very slightly.

Mr. Handsome, his brain still in overdrive, said, "So if you're new, it, uh, means you haven't been to school yet, and if you haven't been to school yet, it means you haven't worn those shoes to school yet, and if you haven't worn those shoes to school yet, then people don't realize you're a megadweeb."

"Listen," said Henry, because he was afraid he might actually call Mr. Handsome "Mr. Handsome" out loud if he kept thinking the name in his head, "could you tell me your name?"

"Theotis T. Otis the Third," said Mr. Handsome.

Ordinarily, Henry might've felt sorry for the average bonehead whose parents had given him a name like that. But Theotis T. Otis the Third was clearly no average bonehead, so Henry didn't.

On the other hand, Henry thought maybe he *could* strike a deal with this Theotis. "You know what, Theotis? You've got a point," Henry admitted. "Nobody around here thinks I'm a megadweeb yet. So?"

"So, if you tell me where the scaredy-cat is, his name is Jurgen, I'll let you have my gym shoes, which are in my backpack," said Theotis.

It occurred to Henry that maybe Theotis was smarter than he looked. This deal could really put Henry's quest to be plain back on track. "Sure," he said to himself. "I could borrow Theotis's shoes, and hide these Elktonium monstrosities in the roadside weeds or in a hollow tree. Theotis's shoes would be a little painful, because Theotis appears to wear size thirteen, not fourteen and a half, but physical pain will be minor compared to the psychological torture the kids at school are sure to inflict on me if I show up in what I'm wearing now, not to mention that reporting for gym class in Elktonium shoes would be very unordinary. Plus, after school, I could change back into the Elktonium shoes when I get off the bus and wear them home, and Dad would be none the wiser!"

Henry took a deep breath. He glanced at the trombone

case. "Well," he said to himself, hating to think what he was about to think. "Theotis is going to figure out where Jurgen is sooner or later, so I might as well tell him what he wants to know, and that way at least one of us gets some good out of this situation—"

"The thing is," Theotis was saying, "I like to yank Jurgen's underpants up and, uh, hang them over his ears every morning before school. Gets me in the right frame of mind to, uh, you know, uh, kick off my day."

Henry rubbed his eyes tiredly and said, "Oh, man." Because he really didn't like bullies. In fact, one of the things he used to do back in the old, unordinary days, when he still wore Batman and Robin boxer shorts and green shoes with red wheels in the heels, was thwart them. Using intelligence, wit, and sometimes, when the struggle grew especially vicious, poetry.

Theotis scowled impatiently. To amuse himself, he stepped on Henry's shoe. Even through the Elktonium absorbed much of the pressure, this still hurt. Theotis was one beefy Texan. Henry knew that if he strayed any further from his quest to be just plain plain by standing up to Theotis, the mashed foot could be just the beginning of the suffering.

Theotis snickered. He found mashing Henry's toes

fun! But before he could enjoy any more yuk-yuks at Henry's expense, a small squeak of fear emerged from the trombone case. Evidently, Jurgen had been watching through the air holes, and had seen what was about to happen to Henry.

"I've got issues with you, New Kid," Theotis warned Henry as he turned away and began to pick the lock on the trombone case. "But right now I've got smaller fish to fry."

Theotis got one of the latches open. Jurgen moaned in fright.

"This is a real conundrum," muttered Henry to himself.

"A real what?" snapped Theotis.

Henry tried frantically to think of a way to do what he was about to do without wrecking his quest for plainness. "I—" said Henry.

"Yeah?" asked Theotis.

"I was talking to your girlfriend," Henry said. He had no idea why he'd brought up Theotis's girlfriend. He didn't even know if Theotis *had* a girlfriend. Henry was flying by the seat of his pants.

"You were talking to Shirley?" Theotis said, scratching his perfectly round head.

"Yeah," said Henry quickly. "*Shirley*. And *Shirley* said . . ."

"What did Shirley, uh, say?" asked Theotis. His attention was starting to wander back toward the trombone case, which rocked to and fro and groaned softly.

"Shirley said, well, she said she really likes that charming lock of blond hair that sticks up three-quarters of an inch from your forehead," declared Henry.

"I *know* that," said Theotis. "*Everybody* likes the lock of hair." He stroked it smugly.

"But you know what she likes even more?" said Henry.

"No, what?" said Theotis.

Now, Henry didn't know Theotis's girlfriend, Shirley. He'd just moved to town. He'd never seen Shirley, or spoken to her, and the only reason he knew her name was that Theotis had just told it to him. For all Henry knew, Shirley was nine feet tall, green, walked on all fours, and had an enormous horn growing out of her forehead. But he didn't let that stop him. No, Henry went right ahead and said, "Shirley told me she likes you because, uh . . . when you send her a text, you call her . . ."

A gaggle of kids flocked up to the bus stop at that moment and gathered to watch.

Theotis turned red as a fire truck and all the air seemed

to leak out of him. He forgot about extracting Jurgen from the trombone case for whatever nefarious purposes he had in mind. "She. Didn't. Tell. You. That?" Theotis croaked, glancing in horror at the crowd of onlookers surrounding him.

"Uh-huh," said Henry smugly. "She did. Shirley told me about . . ."

"Snookums?" wailed Theotis in horror.

"Snookums," repeated Henry.

"Snookums!" cried the mob of kids in glee.

Giggles came out of the gaggle, and a snort even came from the trombone case. Theotis ran away red-faced and hid in the nearest shrubbery he could find.

The bus roared up. Henry rapped on the alligator hide. It scraped his knuckles.

Jurgen leaped out of his trombone case, threw it over his shoulder, ran up the steps, sat right behind the driver where the security camera would catch anybody who tried to smack him, and made himself small.

Henry sat across the aisle, jamming his feet underneath the seat so nobody could see his shoes.

The driver pulled into traffic.

As each block slid past outside the window, Jurgen sat up just a smidgen straighter. Finally, two bus stops later, he called across the aisle to Henry, "I'm starting fifth grade."

"I'm starting sixth," said Henry over his shoulder, and made a point of staring out the window. But as he peered at each of the eleven 7-Elevens lining the road from his house to his new school, trying to remember exactly which one his dad worked at, he kept seeing the reflection of Jurgen sitting across the aisle gazing at the back of his head.

Finally, Jurgen blurted out, "Wow. Oh, man. Did you ever fix him! How do you know his girlfriend, Shirley?"

Henry turned to face Jurgen.

"I don't," said Henry. "I just waited until Theotis let her name slip, and then I acted like I already knew it."

"Good thinking," Jurgen said.

"Thanks," said Henry.

"But how'd you know about 'Snookums'?" asked Jurgen.

"I didn't know about that, either," said Henry. "But usually, when you get somebody as mean, egotistical, and self-centered as Theotis T. Otis the Third talking, he'll embarrass himself. The trick is to pay attention and make sure that when he does, he embarrasses himself a *lot*."

"Immensely," said Jurgen.

"Enormously," said Henry.

"Magnificently," said Jurgen.

"Majestically," said Henry.

"Colossally!" said Jurgen. "Phew!" Jurgen glanced over at Henry with a big grin on his face.

Henry could feel tendrils of friendship reaching out from Jurgen. He thought about sending a tendril or two back. Jurgen Mintfarm was definitely an oddball, but he seemed like Henry's type of oddball.

Or, rather, Jurgen *would* have been Henry's type of oddball, if Henry weren't currently on a mission to achieve plainness. A mission that called for zero oddballs. Weirdness, differentness, or strangeness of any kind could very quickly wreck a quest like Henry's. No, this was a road Henry felt pretty sure he'd be better off traveling without Jurgen Mintfarm.

And so, as the bus sat at a traffic light, Henry focused his attention on a guy beside the road setting up traffic cones for no apparent reason other than keeping cars from running over the guy setting up traffic cones, who was him: the guy setting up traffic cones. *Now that*, thought Henry, *looks like a good way to achieve plainness. As well as being entirely futile.*

After a while, Jurgen quit looking at Henry. He

scrunched up like a potato bug in its segmented shell and stared at the floor as they rode the rest of the way to school in silence, and Henry felt a small kernel of loneliness lodge firmly in his throat. He told himself it was a small price to pay for glorious ordinariness.

The History of a Terrible Haircut

About Henry's quest to be just plain plain: He wasn't undertaking it because he admired the Amish (often known as "the Plain People"). He wasn't planning to turn in all his zippers, grow a beard with no mustache to go with it, wear a big straw hat, and begin riding a buggy to the horse-feed store. In fact, for most of his life, Henry had been pretty much the opposite of plain. Outrageous. Audacious. Disputatious. When he got excited, which he did quite often, his giant black eyes glittered so enthusiastically that you couldn't help liking him, even if he was telling some far-fetched story that had almost no basis in reality, which was another thing he did frequently.

Strange as it may sound, Henry looked a lot like his mother, Melissa, who'd also had size fourteen-and-a-half feet (although she'd been a foot taller than he was—six-four). Their eyes were alike, and they'd both been bald as cue balls. His mother because she was sick. Henry because he had shaved his skull after a particularly awful rainy day in Philadelphia. A storm had driven him off the basketball court at Starr Garden, and Henry had come home dripping wet to find his mother vacuuming the carpet in the dark—all the lights off, all the blinds drawn. Needless to say, her vacuuming wasn't going too well. In the dark, she kept running into the furniture.

Henry tried to sneak past her in the dimness and make for the stairs to his room before he got roped into doing chores. But somehow his mother heard him over the noise of the Bissell. "Henry?" she called. "Can you help me?"

His father was off at the Free Library looking things up for a living. So Henry really had no *choice* but to help. Which made him a little mad. Because, come on! Like most people, he had his own stuff to do. But the tone of his mother's question, a bit timid, a bit scared, even maybe a bit ashamed, so very different from her usual audacious and loquacious voice, made him absolutely furious, which baffled him.

"Just turn on a light, Mom!" Henry shouted.

"I can't," she whispered.

"Then I will," said Henry.

"Oh, Henry," said his mother.

But by then, Henry had turned the light on. And he saw why she wanted to work in the dark. Her treatments had made her hair fall out overnight. She was completely bald.

"Just one of life's little surprises," his mother said nonchalantly, her glittering black eyes now sad and downcast.

Henry couldn't look at her. He muttered, "Maybe you'll get one of those vacuum cleaners with a headlight in it for Christmas." And he ran upstairs.

But Henry's mom didn't get a vacuum cleaner with a headlight in it for Christmas, because she died before Christmas, before Henry could tell her he was sorry for what he'd said, or to help her vacuum. The one thing he did do in time was go to Pietro's Barber Shop and get his cranium shaved, hoping that his mother would guess why: because he was sorry for how he'd acted on that rainy afternoon and was too sad to think of any way to tell her.

All this had taken place eight months before, in Philadelphia, which was full of old trees with millions of green leaves and important brick buildings, before Henry moved to Pumpjack, Texas, which was flat, hot, dusty, and smelled like baking telephone poles.

Henry was *still* bald, and a bald kid is not exactly a plain kid, but apart from that, he was doing his best to cut out all the other audacious, outrageous, disputatious nonsense left over from the old days.

Why?

Because he wanted mealtimes to be more cheerful. Day after day, as Henry and his dad sat across the kitchen table from each other in Pumpjack, eating Frosted Mini-Wheats for breakfast, lunch, and dinner, he saw sadness steal over Phil's face each time their eyes met, because he reminded his dad of Melissa. Henry sometimes felt like an electronic billboard flashing: "She's gone! She's gone! She's gone!"

He hoped that if he stuck to his quest, avoiding anything nutty, kooky, outrageous, audacious, or pugnacious, and instead became boring, then at least his personality wouldn't resemble his mother's so much, so maybe the sad looks on his father's face would fade. Henry's mom used to be a handful, always discovering new metals and performing wild experiments with the time-space continuum, coming up with crazy ideas, imagining things that'd never been imagined before, and Henry used to be a handful, too, like for instance the time he'd convinced a girl at Fairmount Park that the three pinto beans he happened to have in his pocket were actually his adenoids, and sold them to her for six dollars apiece. How was he supposed to know her dad was the new vice principal?

Well, that sort of behavior was officially a thing of the past. Now Henry and Phil lived together in their new house, making three meals a day of breakfast cereal supplemented by simple snack pastries from the wire rack by the 7-Eleven counter, along with the occasional strip of beef jerky. When they weren't eating, they tripped over Elktonium inventions all day long, and they never, ever vacuumed, and neither one knew what to say to the other.

About a Bone

As soon as Henry stepped down from the bus at school, people began noticing his Elktonium shoes. The first kid to say anything was a girl with eleven earrings and a voice like a hyena with its nose caught in a vise. Henry could tell she was stuck-up just by the way she carried her head on her neck—she looked like, so far in her life, her parents had dropped about fifteen thousand bucks taking her to El Paso for ballet lessons and she wasn't going to let anybody forget it.

In his mind, Henry named her "the Arrogant Queen."

"Yaaaah!" the Arrogant Queen said. "What's wrong with your feet?" In the school yard, about ninety pairs of eyes turned to see what was wrong with Henry's feet.

How? Henry asked himself. *How can I explain these shoes without seeming outrageous, audacious, or ostentatious?*

How can I just be—plain boring? But then his mouth opened, and Henry started talking, and these questions faded into the scenery. He said to the Arrogant Queen: "It's not my feet. It's my legs."

"What's wrong with your legs?" asked the Arrogant Queen.

"My legs have no bones," blurted Henry. *Oof,* he scolded himself. *Not plain. Try again.*

"Why not?" the Arrogant Queen asked.

Henry looked around. People were gathering.

"Because my father removed them," Henry exclaimed. *Yikes. Not ordinary. Do over! Do over!*

"What?" shrieked the Arrogant Queen. But she sounded intrigued.

"My father removed my leg bones, because my leg bones had become quite painful," burst out Henry. *Henry,* he told himself, *you just exited the realm of the inconspicuous.* But he didn't know how to turn himself back.

"No way!" said the Arrogant Queen with something like esteem in her voice.

"Actually, he's been removing them one by one for the past four months," Henry said, "and replacing them with an indestructible space-age material developed for Kuala Lumpur's secret astronauts." Regretfully looking back on all this later, Henry figured right about here was where he got so wrapped up in his story that he completely forgot about being unremarkable.

"I've never heard of any astronauts from Kuala Lumpur," said the Arrogant Queen.

"Because they're secret!" shot back Henry.

"Oh, right," murmured the Arrogant Queen.

"Besides," continued Henry, "have you ever heard of Kuala Lumpur?"

"Well," said the Arrogant Queen, who generally spent geography class surfing fashionable shoes on her iPhone, "no."

Henry nodded wisely.

"Hold it! Wait! Not so fast!" the Arrogant Queen shouted. "I don't believe your dad removed your leg bones."

"I don't expect you to believe my dad removed my leg bones," said Henry. "I don't expect anybody to believe my dad removed my leg bones. That's why I brought one for show-and-tell."

"You did not!" whispered the Arrogant Queen.

Slowly, coolly, calmly, collectedly, Henry reached into his Elktonium lunch box and, smiling his widest smile, extracted Pim Pom's bone. The crowd gasped and moved back a step.

"Now, because I have no leg bones—or because, actually, my leg bones are now made of a space-age polymer—my father made these special shoes from Elktonium, a new metal my mother invented, to support my shins in their delicate state." The crowd murmured its approval, and Henry made a mental note to mention "Elktonium support shoes" to his dad at dinner. Maybe orthopedic footwear was the undiscovered purpose of Elktonium, although it seemed like yet another long shot at best.

While he had the crowd's attention, Henry threw in, "Lunch box is Elktonium, too," as if Elktonium shoes were nothing special. "Also the glasses. Not to mention my trumpet." He patted the case.

"Cool!" piped Jurgen in his tiny little voice.

Immediately, Henry felt bad. Not because his quest was running off the rails, since he was way too worked up to notice. And not because he was messing with the mind of the Arrogant Queen, since she was an obnoxious bozo. But Jurgen—Jurgen deserved better than this nonsense.

"Hey, Henry," said Jurgen. "Can I take your leg bone to show-and-tell?"

Henry *really* didn't want to involve Jurgen in the tale

he was so unwisely telling scads of strangers. Even if he and Jurgen weren't destined to be friends, there was no reason to implicate him in whatever fallout was bound to result.

"Um, Jurgen, *I* was going to take it to show-and-tell," said Henry quickly. "Can't really, uh, let you have it." He slipped the bone back into his lunch box.

"Henry," Jurgen said, "you're in sixth grade. I don't know what they used to do at your old school, but at *this* school sixth graders don't *have* show-and-tell!"

"Yeah, Henry," said the Arrogant Queen.

"Yeah, Henry," roared the crowd.

"Come on, Henry," Jurgen said.

"Come on, Henry," said the Arrogant Queen.

"Come on, Henry," said the crowd.

Jurgen looked like he might cry. "I'll give you all my lunch money," said Jurgen.

Henry looked around at the mob. And realized there was no way out of the fib he'd just told. "OK, Jurgen," he said. "But don't lose this. My father might want to put it back someday." Hating himself, Henry handed over the "leg bone." "You can keep your lunch money," he added quietly. "This one's on me."

The Arrogant Queen put her arm around Henry

and said, "So. You're new?"

Henry nodded.

The Arrogant Queen said, "My name's Shirley."

"Oh, no," muttered Henry. "It can't be."

"I'm sorry? I didn't hear that," chirped Shirley.

"You don't by any chance know a guy named Theotis . . . ," Henry asked.

"Theotis? Theotis T. Otis the Third? He's my boyfriend," said Shirley proudly. "Hey. Are you going to take that hat off before you go inside?"

Sometime after lunch, Jurgen Mintfarm was found hanging from a stepladder by his undershorts in the visitors' end zone, near a can of yellow paint.

Seems that a certain *handsome* fellow had gotten the big idea to score a few extra-credit points in science class by bringing in a genuine human leg bone to show around. So the aforementioned handsome fellow (namely Theotis T. Otis the Third) had forcibly removed the leg bone from the custody of its rightful owner (the aforementioned Jurgen Mintfarm).

Imagine Theotis T. Otis the Third's surprise when the science teacher informed him he was trying to score points using a dog's chew toy. Imagine his embarrassment.

Imagine his anger. Imagine his *issues*.

Imagine Theotis dragging Jurgen out to the edge of the football field at approximately 12:57 p.m., right after he finished his lunch.

Imagine a crowd, including Shirley Tantrum, gathering to watch.

Imagine the look in Theotis's eyes when Jurgen, small, friendless, alone, and in danger, tried the "Snookums" trick on him again, only, in his fright, forgot the name "Snookums" and blurted out "Noodles" instead!

Imagine Theotis saying, "Noodles? Who the heck is Noodles?" as he drew back his throwing arm and bounced the dog bone off Jurgen's forehead.

Imagine the various emotions crossing Shirley's face as she witnessed this scene!

Henry imagined it all. He had study hall last period, which gave him fifty-five minutes in which to pull his Phillies cap over his eyes and let his fancy run wild. As the bell rang, Henry asked himself, *Why is everybody and everything who comes in contact with me instantly cursed? How come they all end up shivering in the shrubbery or hanging by their underpants, or immeasurably sad, or worse? Jurgen was better off without me. Ordinariness and friendlessness are my destiny!*

The bell rang. Henry skipped the bus ride and walked home, but not before he circled around the end of the football field and picked up the bone from beneath the visitors' goalpost.

Pim Pom Returns

When Henry got back from school, the toaster was lying in the yard. This happened once in a while. Henry would come home and find it there, sprawled on its side in the dust, soaking up the sun. Its skinny black cord trailed behind it like the tail of an Elktonium kitty cat. If he didn't know better, Henry would've thought it'd walked outside on its own little black plastic feet.

But the logical explanation was that his dad must've left it there as part of some kooky Elktonium experiment he'd forgotten about almost as soon as he'd dreamed it up.

Henry took the toaster inside, plugged it in, and jammed a Jelly Jump-Up down it. Even though his dad hadn't put a knob on the side to control the darkness of each toast/toaster pastry/bagel/waffle, the nice thing about this toaster was, it always got your item just right. Almost as if, due to some unknown property of Elktonium, it could read your mind. The toaster could toast up to four peoples' Jelly Jump-Ups in its four different slots at the same time, and get them *all* right, even if one guy was a light-toaster, like Henry's dad, one guy was a dark-toaster, like Henry, one guy fell somewhere in between, and the last guy was basically a fan of charcoal.

Toasted, the Jump-Up jumped.

Startled, Henry started.

And realized his dad was standing right behind him.

"Oh man!" cried Henry. "I didn't know you were home!"

"It was a slow afternoon at the 7-Eleven," said his dad. "So Roger let me off early. He also sent jerky. Slim Jim brand. The best." Phil produced several packages of beef jerky from his pocket. "It's out-of-date, but that's OK, because this stuff contains more preservatives than most mummies."

Silence fell. Henry buttered his Jelly Jump-Up.

"That's a good idea," said his father.

"What?" asked Henry.

"Dinner," said his dad.

"But it's only three forty-five," began Henry. "I was

just having a snack—"

His dad had already opened the freezer, and was poking around among empty Frozen Eggly Waffle boxes. An Elktonium ice-cube tray slid out. Due to an unfortunate property of its crystal structure, Elktonium became as brittle in the freezer as a three-week-old vanilla wafer, but was about thirty-five times heavier. The ice-cube tray hit Phil's toe, leaving a bruise, and bounced off. Then it clipped the corner of the stove and shattered all over the floor.

Henry's dad solemnly swept the shards into a dustpan and zipped them in a ziplock and put them back in the freezer for safekeeping. This is how things were: Elktonium-related cleanups were just part of daily life at Henry's house.

Henry realized that to other people, bringing so many pointless Elktonium contraptions from Philadelphia in a U-Haul and stashing them in questionable places until they became hazards might've seemed like a dubious idea at best. But to his dad, it made perfect sense. Elktonium was Melissa's proudest creation, so what choice did he have but to treasure every smithereen?

Once the linoleum was clean, Henry located a couple of muffins stored in the crisper (eating only breakfast food cut down on the amount of decision-making he and his dad had to do around the house), and he put the muffins on two Elktonium plates. He dug two Elktonium forks out of the bread box, and together, he and his dad set the so-called meal on the table.

Henry's dad smiled at him. Underneath his smile lay sadness. Henry almost wished his father would give up on the smile and let the sadness show right through, because watching him paste the smile *over* the sadness was actually worse than seeing straight sadness. He could tell his father was watching him and seeing—Melissa.

"I got an interesting call from the school psychologist right before you came home," ventured Henry's dad. "Mrs. Skandar, I think, was her name. Something about a leg bone and a little boy hanging from the goalpost?"

"It wasn't the goalpost. Just a ladder somebody was using to paint the goalpost," said Henry. "I started telling a story. A misunderstanding resulted."

"Was the story outrageous?" asked his father cautiously.

"You could say that, Dad," said Henry.

"Aha," said his father, smiling more brightly, yet more sadly, than ever. "Just try to keep it under control."

"Believe me, Dad," said Henry, "I am."

"Say, were the shoes a hit?" his dad asked, briskly changing the subject.

"A hit?" repeated Henry. Well, they hadn't exactly *been* a hit. They'd gotten *Jurgen* hit. But Henry didn't figure his dad would be too happy to hear that.

Henry's father kept looking at him expectantly. Henry tried to think of a way to say "complete and utter disaster" kindly. But he couldn't. "No, Dad," he replied softly. "They weren't."

"Oh," said Henry's dad, looking disappointed. He stood up from the table and held out his arms. Henry unlaced the shoes and handed them over. "Well, now that dinner is done, I suppose I'll go clear out space on the shelves downstairs to display this Elktonium prototype," his father added sadly.

"Dinner isn't done, Dad," said Henry. "We haven't even started dinner." But Phil didn't seem to hear. He smiled distractedly and shuffled down the basement steps. Henry heard him stumble over the large Elktonium pyramid stored at the bottom of the stairs, and then Henry heard him archive the shoes, one more Elktonium flop condemned to the cellar.

As he sat at the table by himself poking his frigid muffin with a mushy Elktonium fork, wondering if it would be worthwhile warming it up or if he should just gnaw on it the way it was, Henry heard the sound of barking at the back door. He went to look. Of all dogs, it was Pim Pom. "Hey, Pim Pom!" said Henry. Pim Pom capered around on his three legs, pretty much exactly as jubilantly as he'd have capered if he'd had four. "Hold on," said Henry. "I've got your bone!" Henry threw his muffin in the trash, grabbed a banana from the microwave, which was where his dad stored them because the fruit bowl had an Elktonium reciprocating saw in it, and dug Pim Pom's bone out of his backpack. He slid on his jumbo Converse All Star low-tops and slipped outside.

In the dry leaves of the shrubberies, desert crickets scritched tiredly into silence and the brittle desert vines rattled in the breeze.

Henry paused to consider what he was about to do. Make a friend? Was that wise? But Pim Pom was just a shaggy little golden-brown dog. There was no way making friends with a shaggy little golden-brown dog could derail his quest for plainness, right? Ordinary people befriended shaggy little golden-brown dogs every day! He tossed the bone.

But he only tossed it six inches. Pim Pom pounced on it with his one front paw and began to chew.

"No," Henry said. "You're supposed to bring it back. Like this." He took the bone again and drew back to throw. Pim Pom yelped in alarm and began to creep away from Henry. "Are you afraid, boy?" Henry asked. Pim Pom pressed his quivering little body against Henry's leg, and Henry picked him up. Pim Pom tried to burrow into his chest.

"Did something happen? Does fetch scare you?"

At the word "fetch," Pim Pom whimpered.

"Did you get hurt playing fetch?" asked Henry, cradling the tiny dog in his arms. Pim Pom licked Henry's hand. Henry visualized a terrible scene, a negligent owner, a throw gone wrong, a bone bouncing into the street, Pim Pom chasing it, a car appearing out of nowhere. A crash. A shattered leg. He shivered.

"Don't worry," said Henry, setting Pim Pom down and producing a shard of jerky from his pocket. Pim Pom went nuts. He loved beef jerky.

So Henry split a piece with him. Pim Pom loved it so much, Henry tossed him another.

This one, Pim Pom decided to bury. Pim Pom's hole didn't turn out to be much, since the desert was hard and Pim Pom only had one front paw. It was more like a little crater in the ground with a strip of jerky plainly visible in the middle. But Henry didn't want to hurt Pim's feelings, since Pim appeared to be a terrier, a canine noted for its ability to dig. So he pretended not to see the jerky and said, "Excellent burying, Pim Pom!"

Pim Pom grinned at him.

"Listen," said Henry. "Let's stay in the yard to play fetch. You'll be safe. I promise." Henry tossed the bone two feet. And then he got down on all fours, tucked one arm behind his back (so he'd be on all threes, like Pim Pom), scampered over, and picked the bone up in his teeth.

And brought it back to Pim Pom! Pim Pom cocked his head. Now *there* was a twist! This boy was playing fetch! And nothing bad was happening to him!

Henry threw the bone again. Six feet this time. Pim Pom chased it and brought it back. He wagged his stub of a tail! Fetch was fun!

"Hey," said Henry. "How about another slab of jerky?"

"RAAAARF!" replied Pim Pom enthusiastically.

After short break to enjoy more beef jerky, Henry tossed the bone again.

Sometime during the subsequent game of fetch, Phil came out on the back porch to watch. A grin of such true happiness spread over his face that it would've looked dopey if it hadn't been so darned joyful. Suddenly, Phil startled Henry by shouting, "Hey! I've got an idea!"

"What?" said Henry, jumping a foot in the air.

"Maybe that little dog would like to live with us."

Henry pretended to think this over as he wiped dog slobber on his pants—not a whole lot, because Pim Pom wasn't a whole lot of dog. He fought down the excitement that was welling up inside his rib cage, struggling to jam it back into his pancreas, or wherever it'd come from. Pim Pom? His dog? Living at his house? "OK," he replied. "Sure. Maybe. But what if his owner is looking for him?"

Henry's dad checked the license hanging from Pim Pom's collar. "Expired six months ago," he said. "His owner isn't looking for him. He's looking for an owner." After a thoughtful pause, he added, "Hey, Henry—know what'd make a good doghouse?"

Henry thought about it. "That crazy Elktonium pyramid at the bottom of the basement stairs, the one Mom made, that you never get rid of even though there's really no place to store it?"

"That very one!" said his dad.

"It's already hollow," said Henry, following his dad inside and downstairs, "so all we need to do is cut a door in one side using the hacksaw blade of my pocket-sized

Titanium Technical Tool. . . ." Henry's voice trailed off. Usually, the mention of Henry's Titanium Technical Tool threw his dad into a funk. Titanium, being a strong, useful metal, represented everything that Elktonium was not, so it was the enemy, as far as Phil Cicada was concerned. The fact that Henry would consider using a tool made of titanium probably would've hurt Phil's feelings deeply, if he hadn't been so darned stoked about building an Elktonium doghouse.

Quickly, before the mood had a chance to change, Henry sawed an arched opening in the pyramid. It was shaped much like the door in Snoopy's house. Henry and his dad dragged the pyramid into the yard. "Time to move into your new home!" said Phil to Pim Pom, but Pim only sniffed at the pyramid warily. *Gah!* It smelled of tropical Mr. Clean: mango, coconut, and disinfectant. Dogs hate and fear this. Which was a fact Henry and Phil had lost sight of in their enthusiasm.

Off Pim Pom ran into the bushes.

"Come on! Try out your new house!" coaxed Phil.

"Come on, Pim Pom! Come on!" said Henry.

"This is exactly the kind of thing your mom would've done," observed Phil, his voice growing shaky. "She loved three-legged dogs."

As soon as his dad said this, Henry realized it was true. In her free time, Melissa used to be outrageously kind to injured animals, splinting the broken wings of birds, sewing tiny eye patches for half-blind squirrels, and building minuscule carts for guinea pigs with fractured legs to roll themselves around in. Wow. Just when Henry thought it was safe to get excited about something (for instance, a three-legged puppy), it wasn't.

Besides, try as they might, neither Henry nor his dad could persuade Pim Pom to come out of the bushes. Henry thought he could see the disappointment in his dad's eyes. Henry's dad thought he could see the disappointment in Henry's. And as they stared at each other, the disappointment, which hadn't necessarily been real at first, became very real indeed.

"Well," said Henry's dad. "I have a hunch that the Elktonium fruit cup will prove to be a hit, as long as nobody serves lemons in it. So I guess I'll go work on that." Shoulders sagging, he trudged back inside, leaving Henry in the yard alone.

A Blinding Flash of Fruity Light

Henry's kernel of loneliness reemerged right about then, pulsing like a heartbeat three inches below his Adam's apple, in that hollow at the base of the neck that, if you poke it with your finger, makes you cough.

Henry poked the kernel, the way you sometimes poke a bruise, to see what'll happen, like will it hurt, or what? In this case, the poke made Henry cough. And cough and cough. Boy, had that poke been a miscalculation. It took three long, miserable, teary-eyed minutes for the hacking to stop. But when he could breathe again, Henry developed a steely, determined look in his eyes, and he stood up straight and squared his shoulders, as if preparing to take an important step. "You know what?" Henry said to himself. "I'm tired of this stupid kernel of loneliness."

He marched over to the prickly asphalt-scented desert shrubbery, reached in, extracted Pim Pom, and set him down in the yard on his three sturdy legs. He knew making friends with Pim might remind his dad of all kinds of sad things associated with Melissa, but . . .

. . . Henry picked up Pim Pom's bone anyway. To take Pim Pom's mind off his instinctive canine fear of Elktonium, Henry dangled the bone above Pim's nose. When Pim Pom jumped for it, Henry lifted the bone just out of reach. Pim Pom danced excitedly on his hind legs. Henry twirled the bone in circles, and made Pim Pom spin like a tiny cyclone, yipping like mad. He was not teasing the little dog. He was merely heightening Pim Pom's anticipation. When Pim Pom was nothing but two gleaming eyes and a flapping tongue, Henry drew back his arm, hollered "Fetch," and flung the bone toward the doghouse.

At that moment, the rays of the setting sun happened to hit the Elktonium surface of the new doghouse at very low angle: a hair under seven degrees. While the bone flew toward its door, Henry noticed the shimmering iridescent green surface of the doghouse becoming agitated. Tiny points of chartreuse light pulsed and skittered around the sides and ran up and down, settling into some kind of rhythm, some kind of pattern, almost like they were flashing a message in code. At the top of the doghouse, Henry could swear the image of an eyeball began to take shape. It looked like the eyeball atop the pyramid on the dollar bill in your pocket.

Eerie.

The bone rattled through the door.

Pim Pom charged after it, his ears cocked at attention.

"Pim Pom!" cried Henry. "Stop!"

Just as the sun dropped to the cottonwood treetops in the yard next door, its rays striking the doghouse at an angle of a smidgen over six degrees, the bone flew through the door of the Elktonium pyramid. Pim Pom skidded into the doghouse an instant after the bone. There was a flash of strawberry-tangerine-colored light, after which the house (and the dog and bone inside it) disappeared.

"Pim Pom?" said Henry. "Fella?"

No answer.

"Here, doggy," said Henry, creeping toward the empty spot in the yard where Pim Pom, his bone, and his doghouse had last been. Gone. Definitely all gone. Doghouse, dog, and bone.

Henry couldn't believe it. Sure, this was the kind of thing he used to make up and tell people about, but it wasn't the kind of thing that really happened.

"Pim Pom?" he called. "Pim Pom?" He felt panic beginning to creep up his spine and tickle his ribs from the inside. "Doggy? Where'd you go?"

Nothing. No answer.

This, thought Henry, *is what I get for trying to make friends.* But before he could feel much sadder or sorrier for himself, Henry's dad cranked open the basement ventilation grate, and through it he called, "Did Pim Pom go into his house?"

Henry figured if his dad had been sad when Pim Pom wouldn't go in the doghouse, it probably wouldn't make him feel much better to learn that when Pim Pom finally *had* gone into the doghouse, he'd been instantaneously snatched from the face of the earth in a blinding flash of fruity light, which would not only dishearten him, but also carry very strong overtones of outrageousness and remind him of Melissa. And so, luckily, Henry stopped worrying about his own feelings and started worrying about his dad's. This kept him from being overwhelmed by sadness, and it kept his brain working pretty smoothly.

"Uh, yeah," said Henry. "Dad, Pim Pom *did* go into the house."

"How does he like it?" asked Henry's dad.

"He found it very *interesting*!" Henry replied. "I feel sure."

"Oh, good," said his father, "I'm glad Pim Pom is so interested in his house," and he got back to work.

Henry breathed a quick sigh of relief, gave thanks that his dad's workaholism had once again protected him from the truth, and sat in the fading sunlight feeling very, very alone. The kernel of loneliness now felt like a pomegranate. But he refrained from poking it. Henry knew that in a few minutes, he'd have to make up some kind of story explaining Pim Pom's disappearance, not to mention the disappearance of the Elktonium doghouse. Maybe he could tell his father that a little old lady had arrived out of the blue driving a Ford pickup to say that Pim Pim actually belonged to her. Yes! He could say the little old lady had put Pim Pom in the front seat of her truck to take him home, and she'd liked the doghouse so much she put it in the back and took it, too!

That might work. He could invent a joyful reunion scene between Pim Pom and his fictitious former master and act really pleased as he recounted how the whole thing had gone down. That way, his father wouldn't have to worry about any of this, and could go on making himself happy by fashioning useless items out of

Elktonium in the basement.

Which, of course, wouldn't make Henry feel much better, or make him miss Pim Pom any less: how his fur smelled freshly baked when the sun hit it, the way he smiled with his pointy little teeth, and how his whole body wagged when he was happy since his tail was nothing but a formality.

But lo and behold, just when it seemed like Pim Pom might be gone forever, the Elktonium pyramid rematerialized. Henry heard the sound of a dog bone clattering around inside, and then out it tumbled. "Pim Pom!" cried Henry. "Here, puppy! Here!" In the sky, the strawberry-tangerine light of the sunset achieved its brightest intensity yet, and the doghouse shimmered furiously as the eyeball on top stared at Henry. And then, Henry could swear, the eye winked at him right before Pim Pom came spilling out the door.

"What," muttered Henry, "is going on? What's in there, Pim Pom? Where did you go? What did you see?"

Pim Pom didn't answer, but his wide eyes, quivering tail stub, and shaky legs told Henry that whatever Pim Pom had experienced, it'd been sorta wild.

Above them, the sun hung at an angle of 5.62 degrees, which still rounds up to six.

The eye at the top of the pyramid swiveled around and stared straight at Henry. It lifted its brow challengingly. It seemed to be daring him to jump inside and find out for himself what went on in there.

OK.

Resolutely, Henry stalked backward across his yard. He came to the shrubbery at the edge. He stopped. Pressing down on him, he felt sadness, loneliness, and boredom. He also felt the bus stop, the Arrogant Queen, Mr. Handsome, and the relentless diet of breakfast food. He dug his feet into the dirt for traction—he wanted to get a good start. Then Henry Cicada took a deep breath and started running—running right out from underneath everything that weighed him down, until, two yards from the doghouse, sprinting for all he was worth, he dove headfirst through the door of the glittering, glimmering, shimmering pyramid, and into—he didn't know what; he didn't care—all he hoped was that wherever the doghouse took him, it'd be different from Pumpjack, and it wouldn't smell of creosote. Pim Pom leaped in behind him. For a split second, nothing happened. And then, as the sun shone down from an angle of 5.61 degrees, which still plainly rounds up to six, Henry, Pim Pom, and the pyramid all disappeared in a flash of—yes, that's right—strawberry-tangerine light.

From a darkened window next door, a whiskery old man who'd once led thousands of troops into battle watched everything through narrowed eyes, and in the basement of Henry's house, a shaft of sunlight found its way through the ventilation grate and bathed Phil Cicada's Elktonium key fob in a cosmic pool of brilliance.

The Firebird!

While his son was outside quietly disappearing to who knew where, Phil Cicada gazed in wonder at the sunlit key fob on his workbench. He set down his awl. He pushed aside his rasp and his mattock. He hung his adze on his pegboard. For a spellbound moment, Phil let himself forget about inventing Elktonium contrivances and just plain enjoyed the strange beauty of the pixelating metal in front of him. This was behavior he'd never before observed in Elktonium!

The wonder of the spectacle before him made Phil so curious that he forgot about finding the true purpose of Elktonium. Instead, he turned to what he knew best: looking stuff up. Only instead of looking for information in the stacks of the Free Library of Philadelphia like he used to, Phil plugged in Melissa's scanning quarktronic microscope, a handy tool he'd brought from Philadelphia in the U-Haul just in case, and looked for information hidden in the structure of Elktonium itself. What, he wondered, was causing this extraordinary pixelation?

Through the unprecedentedly powerful microscope, the structure of Elktonium looked to Phil a lot like the structure of the universe. Electrons and protons and neutrons and bosons swirled around deep inside Elktonium like minuscule planets and suns and moons arrayed in systems and constellations and galaxies. It was all beautiful, complex, strange, and sort of familiar. It was like looking outward at the infinitely large cosmos, except Phil was looking inward at an infinitely small one. And then he glimpsed a smaller galaxy inside the one he happened to be observing. And a smaller one inside that one.

And as he stared, it began to seem to Phil that in the patterns lay a message. The shaft of sunlight blazing through the grate grew stronger. The Elktonium pulsed, almost as if it were alive. And then Phil began to glimpse its secret. "Holy moly, Melissa," Phil whispered. "Dimensions we've never dreamed of. Places we've never seen. Distances we've never imagined. Risk we can't comprehend. Sadness we've never known. Happiness we've never measured." He tore his eyes away from the screen of the microscope. "Henry!" he hollered through the ventilation grate. "Don't get too close to that doghouse!"

But of course Henry was closer than close to the doghouse. He was inside it. Which felt a lot like being inside his uncle Leon's 1979 Pontiac Firebird when Uncle Leon hit the Atlantic City Expressway bound for the casino, the streetlights nothing but a blurry tunnel of glare as far as the eye could see. Boom! Rocket to Mars! Curled Henry's toes and rattled his eyeballs!

But then, as suddenly as it had begun, the acceleration ceased, and Henry felt himself falling for what seemed like a day and a half, until, finally, he was—

—tumbling out of the pyramid into the driver's seat of an actual 1979 Pontiac Firebird. Pim Pom landed in the passenger seat, and the pyramid wedged itself in back.

Before Henry had a chance to worry too much about any of this, his ears were beset by the screech of collapsing sheet metal. He frantically searched the car's dashboard until he found the headlight knob and set the high beams ablaze. As soon as Henry got the lights on, though, he wished he hadn't, because the first thing he saw were the walls of a metal compactor poised to crush the Pontiac like an aluminum can. Realizing that he had, at best, about four seconds to live, Henry shouted, "Help! Help!"

"Arf! Arf!" echoed Pim Pom. He leaped into Henry's lap and curled up under the steering wheel.

"I am so sorry I got you into this, little dog," cried Henry.

Pim Pom licked his hand. The walls of the metal compactor shuddered and slowed.

"Get me out of here!" yelled Henry. The walls of the metal compactor stopped.

"Please!" he shouted. The hardened steel walls reversed themselves.

Henry noticed the Elktonium doghouse glowing slightly in the backseat of the Firebird. "Thanks for all your help when I was about to be squashed," Henry told it sarcastically. The eye at the top gave him a very cool look and then haughtily directed its attention somewhere over his head as the pyramid hummed ever so faintly in "idle" mode.

"Who said that?" a voice asked. It was a kind voice, kinder than any voice Henry could remember hearing in a long, long time. And as the voice spoke, the walls of the compactor retracted farther and the spiderwebbed cracks in the windshield of the Pontiac slowly repaired themselves and the hood and the fenders of the car eased back into shape.

Henry said, "*I* said that."

The voice said, "Who are you?"

Henry said, "Henry Cicada."

Pim Pom barked.

"That's Pim Pom," added Henry.

"*Where* are you?" said the voice.

"I *was* in Pumpjack, Texas," said Henry. "It's a dusty little town just this side of . . ."

". . . Nowhere," supplied the voice. "I've heard of it. But what I mean is, where are you *now*?"

The walls of the metal compactor receded into the darkness so far that Henry couldn't see them anymore, and they were replaced by the walls of what appeared to be an average one-car suburban garage.

"I'm not sure," said Henry. He felt something poking him in the tailbone. He wormed his hand around, grabbed the something, and scooched it up in front of his face so he could look at it. It was a ballet slipper. A very large one. A huge one, in fact. Maybe size fourteen and a half. "In a car with a ballet slipper on the front seat?" said Henry.

"I love ballet," said the voice. "I especially adore *The Firebird.*"

A premium-brand automatic garage-door opener suddenly appeared on the ceiling and the one-car garage became a two-car garage.

"The Firebird," Henry murmured, patting the dashboard of the Pontiac he was sitting in. "Pure genius." He reminisced for a second about his uncle Leon's hot rod. "Power, beauty, and grace!"

"Exactly!" the voice agreed. "Power, beauty, and grace!"

A handsome green lawn tractor sporting a leaping deer on the hood materialized next to Henry in the garage. Sunshine streamed through the high square windows in the automatic door. Pim Pom leaped into the passenger seat, put his front paw on the dashboard, and peered through the windshield, wagging his tail.

"Yeah," said Henry, who was beginning to figure out that all this talk of Firebirds was somehow responsible for the improved circumstances he was enjoying (from metal crusher to two-car garage with automatic door opener). "Especially the chrome hubcaps."

"The chrome what?" asked the voice in confusion, as the garage walls shuddered and bulged inward and the sun disappeared outside the windows. "What are you talking about?"

"I'm talking about the Firebird!" said Henry, patting the steering wheel. "Power, beauty, and grace!"

"Power, beauty, and grace!" repeated the voice in a brighter tone, and the walls quit collapsing. "That's what I'm talking about, too!"

"Nutty place," muttered Henry under his breath. Then, in a more cheerful tone, he asked, "Hey—what's *your* name?" Maybe, he figured, with more information about his surroundings, he could figure out what in the name of Benjamin Franklin was going on.

"Lulu," the voice said. "Lulu MacDougal."

"Who are you?" Henry said.

"I'm a giant," said Lulu.

"OK," muttered Henry to himself. "This clears a few things up, actually. Sure. I've been under a lot of stress lately, and life has been hard, so what's happening right now is that I'm LOSING MY EVER-LOVING MIND!"

"I'm the Giant Tire Giant of Raisin, Texas," Lulu added. "And you know what's kind of funny?"

"No," replied Henry with a sigh. "But I can only hope you'll tell me."

"It seems like you're maybe, kind of, I don't know—in my thoughts?" she said.

"That's hilarious all right," said Henry.

"Well, I didn't mean funny like that," said Lulu. "I meant 'strange.'"

"Then, Lulu," Henry said, "we're on the same page."

Pim Pom dug an imaginary hole in the automotive carpet with his good paw. Pim Pom *did* have that terrier ancestry in him somewhere, so even though he was missing one digger, he went at it with all his heart. When he was "finished," he crawled imaginatively inside to hide.

"Let's test your theory," proposed Henry. "Lulu, what are you thinking about right now?"

"A boy," said Lulu. "With a bald head. And glittering eyes. Sitting in a car. If I look closely, he's blushing."

"Sounds like me," admitted Henry.

"Wow!" Lulu said. "This hasn't happened in a long time."

"What hasn't happened?" said Henry.

"There's something in my thoughts! There hasn't been *anything* in my thoughts since—I can't think when. And now there's you!" said Lulu. "Plus, an old car. And a lot of tools stored on steel shelving. Why am I thinking about all this? Weird."

"Is that logically even possible?" asked Henry. "To have no thoughts when you think?"

"I don't know if it's logical," mused Lulu, "but it sure happens."

"Sounds awful," said Henry. Pim Pom whined in sympathy.

"It is," said Lulu. "Henry, you sound like the voice in my head. You know, the one that says, 'That cloud looks like an emu,' when a cloud looks like an emu, or, 'Hey, brussels sprouts actually seem to be very small cabbages!' when, at Thanksgiving, you realize brussels sprouts actually seem to be very small cabbages."

"Or the one that says, 'I'd better stop by the bathroom before geography class or I'm gonna be in trouble by the time we get to Djibouti'?" asked Henry.

"Exactly!" said Lulu.

"So obviously, I'm in your imagination," said Henry.

"Obviously," said Lulu. And next to the handsome lawn tractor in the garage, yet another parking stall opened up, this one with a Jaguar parked in it, since imaginations are the kind of thing that, the more you use them, the better they get. "Whoa," said Lulu. "Check out that Jag."

Henry still had a couple of concerns, but he decided to keep them to himself, because he didn't want to hurt Lulu's feelings, or bring the garage walls back down on him again.

First: Even though they'd established that he was in Lulu's imagination, they hadn't established if Lulu was actually *real*, and not just a product of his freaking-out mind.

And second: Even if Lulu *was* real, *where* was she? Henry could only guess where the nutty Elktonium pyramid might've taken him. To the undiscovered planet Spudmotron? In the unexplored Digestive System? Of the as-yet-undetected galaxy Thermidor?

Henry climbed from the car and found a rusty yellow stepladder under the suburban garage's handsome pine workbench. He put it next to the door, climbed up, and looked through the windows. The first thing Henry saw outside was a rattlesnake slithering across the loneliest stretch of desert highway he'd ever seen in any cowboy movie. Then next thing he saw was a buzzard flying past. Then he nearly jumped off the stepladder as some strange kind of shutter dropped over the windows and flew back up in, well . . . the blink of an eye?

Looking through the windows of the garage was like looking through Lulu's eyes! Just as soon as Henry figured this out, there came into view a face. A woman's face. A woman's face that might've been, with a few minor changes, kind of pretty. But it wasn't pretty, because it wore a squinty, sharp, suspicious expression that was kind of horrifying, had been dyed the most eye-popping shade of Tan-Ur-Self self-tanning lotion available at the cosmetics counter at Flor-Mart (burnt orange), and was as wrinkled as the deflated 1963 football stored in the University of Texas trophy case commemorating the Longhorns' national championship that year.

This face smiled the rueful, pasted-on, bitter smile of a woman who was used to getting her way and was prepared to go ballistic in milliseconds when she didn't. In fact, here is the message conveyed by that smile: *I find it amusing that you're even thinking about arguing with me, given the world of hurt I'm prepared to lay on you if you do.* It was possibly the most malevolent smile anyone had ever smiled in Texas.

"Yaaaah!" said Lulu to Henry inside her head. "It's my aunt. Tiffany Glint."

Henry shivered.

"Looolooo?" he heard Tiffany croon. He saw Lulu's eyes blink rapidly as she gazed down at Tiffany Glint. Tiffany stood on the pointy toes of her armadillo-skin cowboy boots and stuck her nose up toward Lulu's. Lulu seemed to be about a foot taller than Tiffany. "Ain't nobody stopped into my tire store all day," Tiffany said. "Any idea why?"

Lulu didn't answer.

"I ain't had all the advantages you've had, honey," Tiffany continued sweetly. "I have not been blessed with your opportunities, and I don't have your sophisticated understanding of what all goes on in the world. BUT I DO KNOW YOU AIN'T BEEN HOLDING YOUR TIRE IN THE AIR!"

Henry felt Lulu's imagination flinch. The floor lurched with a sickening jolt, knocking Henry off the stepladder and onto the hood of the Firebird.

"You out here talking to some kinda imaginary friend?" asked Tiffany, running her lizard-y blue eyes slowly over the landscape. "HUH?"

Henry felt Lulu shake her head. The Jaguar disappeared from the garage. All four tires on the lawn tractor suddenly went flat. The ominous hum of a metal crusher droned somewhere behind the garage walls, which suddenly began to bulge inward.

"I wasn't talking to anybody," said Lulu.

"Wasn't talking to nobody," mocked Tiffany. She laughed a humorless laugh and smiled her malevolent smile. "Well then, why in the diddly doodad have I been sitting in the Giant Tire Emporium office underneath the cool breeze of my window-unit air conditioner watching yore lips moving for the past ten minutes?" Lulu took a step backward and Henry felt her stumble. "Git back on your pile a rocks!" Tiffany hollered like a drill sergeant, or maybe a prison warden. Henry felt Lulu staggering as she climbed upward. "Hold that tire up in the air!" Tiffany Glint screamed, spit flying from her lips. Henry saw the tire go up. "Good!" barked Tiffany. "Now keep it up there."

By now, inside Lulu's imagination, Henry was squeezed so tightly his eyeballs began to squeak in his eye sockets. The hood badge of the Pontiac was making a permanent impression in his derriere, and the extremely large ballet slipper had wedged its nose into the notch of his rib cage. As the walls of Lulu's imagination continued to implode, the shoe seemed to be burrowing toward his spleen.

"Lulu!" Henry shouted. "Lulu!" But it was no use. Tiffany Glint exerted some sort of terrible power over Lulu's mind, causing it to shrink. Henry realized his only hope was to snag Lulu's attention and take her thoughts off Tiffany Glint's derision before her imagination shriveled up to nothing, crushing him and his new friend Pim Pom out of existence.

Dimensions 47, 48, and 49

Meanwhile, to back up a tiny bit, down in Henry's basement, Henry's dad was still hollering at him through the ventilator. "Definitely stay away from the pyramid, Henry," he called. "'Cause I think it could maybe take you . . . somewhere . . . really unusual . . ." His voice trailed off as he directed his attention back to the information hidden in Elktonium's patterned parts. After all, Phil Cicada was skilled at looking up facts, whether they were hidden in the stacks of the Philadelphia Free Library or in the microstructure of a new metal. He made another note. Several of them, in fact. Here they are:

Universes within universes
Worlds within worlds!
There is a connection
between the 1st, 2nd,
and 3rd dimensions
(which we inhabit)
and the

And here in Phil Cicada's notes appears the coffee stain left by his mug when he set it down to count all the dimensions linked together inside the structure of Elktonium. "Five, six, seven, eight," Phil intoned. "Nine, ten, eleven, twelve." He picked up his mug and had another swig of coffee. He rubbed his eyes. Sometimes, history teaches us, all you have to do to learn amazing stuff is to look carefully. And count correctly. "Thirteen, fourteen, fifteen, sixteen," he continued, "seventeen, eighteen, nineteen, twenty . . ."

By the time Phil put his coffee down again, this is what he'd written:

47th, 48th, and 49th dimensions!!!!!!

"Wow," murmured Phil. "There are forty-nine dimensions out there waiting to be explored by some lucky guy who happens to have the right doohickey." He gazed thoughtfully into the crystal structure of Elktonium. "I wonder what things are like in the forty-seventh, forty-eighth, and forty-ninth dimensions?"

Meanwhile, Henry found himself crushed against a deteriorating Firebird, watching through the eyes of a Giant Tire Giant as a green Toyota Clodhopper pulled into the Giant Tire parking lot behind the appalling Tiffany Glint.

"Just great," muttered Tiffany. "The mayor's here. What in the Sam Hill does he want?" Tiffany turned to Lulu. "Take a small breather, Lulu. Put the tire down. The mayor has all kinds of prissy attitudes about child labor."

Turned out, a small breather for Lulu also spelled a small breather for Henry and Pim Pom, who were able to relax once she relaxed, because when she relaxed, her imagination relaxed, so they could breathe, which brings us back to the place where this sentence started, which is a good place to call it quits.

"Good evening, Ms. Glint," began the mayor.

Peering intently through Lulu's eyes, Henry saw that

the mayor of Raisin, Texas, was none other than Hamm Fontaine, former defense tackle for the Dallas Cowboys! When Henry was a kid, Hamm and the rest of the Cowboys used to come to Philadelphia once each fall, where Hamm jammed on his helmet and ran over the Eagles's quarterback like a diesel dump truck for three straight hours. Today, though, despite his former fearsomeness, the mayor removed his Raisin #1 bill cap and twisted it nervously in his hands, shifting from foot to foot and smiling timidly at Tiffany.

"Can I help you?" demanded Tiffany unhelpfully.

"On behalf of the Right On, Raisin! Civic Committee," said Mayor Fontaine, "I just wanted to thank you for the positive attitude you have displayed in what might otherwise have been an unpleasant—"

"Yeah, yeah, yeah," said Tiffany.

"The committee wanted you to understand that their decision in no way reflects their opinion of your perceived talents," continued the mayor.

"Of course not," said Tiffany, rolling her eyes.

"It's just that, when you kindly sent your niece, Lulu, to fill your spot at dress rehearsal—" the mayor plowed on.

"That *was* kind of me, wasn't it?" muttered Tiffany. "I

had a dentist appointment for tooth whitening."

"It was lucky, too," added the mayor, "because while Lulu was doubling for you on the Spirit of Raisin float, the grand marshal, my wife, Bridget Fontaine, with whom you are acquainted, noticed, when the band began to play, that Lulu here performed—what was that awesome dance move you threw down, honey?"

Tiffany shot Lulu a glare from the corner of her eye that made a crack appear in the garage floor under Henry's feet. Lulu didn't answer. Lulu couldn't answer. She seemed to be frozen.

"A ballet step of some sort?" prompted the mayor. "That the grand marshal, my wife, Bridget Fontaine, felt like really, ah . . ." Mayor Fontaine fished a Post-it out of his cowboy shirt. He studied the note inscribed on it. ". . . embodied the uplifting spirit we want to convey, going forward."

"I know," said Tiffany flatly. "She wrote me the same thing in a email."

"The committee wasn't sure if you got that email," said Mayor Fontaine. "Since you didn't answer."

"Oh, I got it, all right," said Tiffany.

"The committee was afraid you might be a bit— upset?" prompted Mayor Fontaine.

"Why would I be upset, Mayor?" wondered Tiffany. "Just because the committee has replaced me with my own niece after I portrayed the Spirit of Raisin on the grand marshal's float every year since 1994?"

"Ah. That was a memorable year. Yes indeed. A memorable year that I remember well," said the mayor, starting to sound more like a mayor. He seemed relieved to be moving on to a discussion of happier times. "I drove the John Deere tractor to which your large rolling raisin was hitched, leading the parade. Boy, howdy, did you twirl your baton fast. It looked like the propeller of the crop duster airplane I used to fly as a teenager when I gunned the engine to avoid low-hanging power lines. I don't even know how you did it. Block after block. Staring fiercely into the distance at something. Something I couldn't see. Every two minutes on the dot, boy, howdy, you flang that baton higher than the top of the water tower. And caught it like a pro."

"Yeah," said Tiffany. "I know. I was there. Every year for twenty-one years. Until it was all brought to a screeching halt." Henry saw her shoot an acid glance toward Lulu.

"Uh-huh. About that," said the mayor. "I guess it's just a little weird to see a thirty-nine-year-old woman up there doing that stuff. Which might have played at least a small role in the committee's decision to offer the role to your niece."

"What?" snapped Tiffany. In one step, she was standing pointy boot toe to pointy boot toe with the mayor, stabbing her nose straight up in the direction of his Adam's apple.

The mayor's mouth clapped shut and a terrified look appeared on his face when he realized he'd just called Tiffany Glint weird.

"It's just that, um, ah," stammered the mayor, backing away as he frantically checked his Post-it note to see if it offered any help, "according to the committee, Lulu's commanding presence in public, not to mention the imagination displayed by her impromptu dancing, and her beauty, grace, and power—"

"You're right," said Tiffany. "No need to mention any of that."

But Henry took it as a good sign that at the mention of the words "beauty, grace, and power," an authentic pair of fuzzy dice began dangling from the Firebird's rearview mirror.

"I mean—" said Mayor Fontaine.

"If there's nothing else?" said Tiffany, grinding her blinding white teeth together as she struggled to wrassle her temper under control. "I got a tire business to run?"

"No, there's nothing else," said the mayor in a relieved voice, stuffing the Post-it back into his pants pocket. Quickly, he wedged himself into his tiny car and glided away on electric power.

"And now," growled Tiffany, turning to Lulu, "that the mayor has been kind enough to bring the subject up, let's just take this opportunity to put all the dang Spirit of Raisin nonsense to bed once and for all."

"I didn't do that dance atop the Raisin float on purpose. I just liked the music. I don't even *want* to be the Spirit of Raisin," Lulu pleaded.

"Good. 'Cause I don't want you to be, either," muttered Tiffany.

"But if the Right On, Raisin! Civic Committee *did* like my dance"—began Lulu, and as she said this, the paint in the garage brightened and the needle of the gas gauge in the Firebird climbed a quarter of a tank, because the thought that was coming to her, Henry could tell, strengthened her resolve—"then maybe there's something about it I should feel proud of?"

"I got two words for you, Lulu," said Tiffany.

"What are they?" asked Lulu.

Henry braced himself for something awful.

"P. P.!" said Tiffany.

Henry thought about whether "P. P." counted as two words. Or any words.

"P. P.?" repeated Lulu.

"Pity privilege!" spat Tiffany disgustedly. "When people feel sorry for you, they give you privileges. Like when they let that little one-legged kid do the honorary kick-off at County Champs? They prop him up on a couple a broomsticks or crutches or whatever so he can kick with his one remaining leg without falling over? 'Cause they feel bad for him. Some people are even crying. And it's due to pity. On the other hand, some are laughing! I know I am!"

"People are laughing?" echoed Lulu.

"Yeah," said Tiffany. "Just like they're laughing at you. 'Cause you are deluded enough to think they're offering you the Spirit of Raisin job due to your talent level."

"But it's really pity?" said Lulu.

"You just hit the gopher on the head!" replied Tiffany. "And now, for an antidote to this situation, I am happy to suggest that you turn your thoughts to undertaking a more appropriate activity than being the Spirit of Raisin: being the Giant Tire Giant. The job description includes silently holding a tire above your head for hours on end, in all weather, day in and day out, the way carpet giants hold a carpet over their heads, and doughnut giants hold a doughnut over their heads, and muffler giants hold a muffler over their heads, so people passing in their cars will see a large human form displaying a retail product high in the air and come purchase it!"

"But why is it more appropriate for me to be a Tire Giant?" implored Lulu.

The floor rumbled and shifted under Henry and Pim Pom as misgivings squeezed Lulu's imagination.

"Why? *Why? WHY* IS BEING A TIRE GIANT MORE APPROPRIATE?" screamed Tiffany. "HOW ABOUT IF I ASK THE QUESTIONS FOR A CHANGE?"

"Yes, Aunt Tiffany," responded Lulu meekly.

"WHY ARE YOU ALWAYS DOUBTING ME?"

"Sorry, Aunt Tiffany," said Lulu. "It's just that—"

"DON'T YOU DOUBT ME!" cried Tiffany. "FIRST, YOU TAKE MY JOB, AND NOW, YOU DOUBT ME!" She took a deep breath and calmed herself down. Somewhat. "Lulu, I think it's far more important to doubt your decision to climb up on the Raisin float and cut pinafores and isotopes and all them froufrou steps. 'Cause that was embarrassing, Lulu. For you! Galumphing around in front of people like a stork with those elbows of yours flying all over the place!"

As the walls crumbled and began to collapse again, Henry saw Tiffany gazing curiously in through Lulu's eyes, as if she were trying to read Lulu's thoughts. And he noticed something odd. From the humongous steerhide handbag draped over Tiffany's shoulder peeked the spine of a book. And even in his deteriorating state, Henry thought this was strange. For at least two reasons: One, Tiffany didn't seem like the type to carry around books of any sort, since she didn't exactly strike him as a big reader. Two, the book was *The BFG* by Roald Dahl.

"*The Big Friendly Giant*," murmured Henry to himself. "What's that all about?"

"Goldarn, Lulu! Gimme a break!" snorted Tiffany Glint. "You go whomping all over town on the Spirit of Raisin float with your knees whizzing through the air like they do, you gonna knock some little spectator cold as a frozen pizza!" Tiffany paused and laughed at the thought. She slapped her knee. She blotted the tears from her eyes, and blew her nose on her fingers. Then she wiped her fingers on her Giant Tire coveralls. When she thought nobody important was watching, Tiffany Glint could be a real pig.

Henry and Pim Pom dove into the car.

The garage shriveled up almost to nothing. Pim Pom nestled forlornly against Henry. Henry's eyesight went dim. He found himself hanging on to consciousness by a thread, his blood hardly moving in his veins, his heart shuddering to a stop, and his nerve endings shorting out. It was all he could do to make it from one gasp of air to the next, and to keep his arms wrapped protectively around Pim Pom's quivering form. "Lulu!" gasped Henry. "Lulu!" But she didn't seem to hear. This was the end of his life, Henry realized. He hadn't even told his father good-bye.

"Goldarnit all, Lulu!" Henry heard Tiffany Glint say outside, as if from a great distance. "Time for you to quit daydreaming and get back to work. Hop to it!"

And since Lulu had almost no imagination at all by this point, she didn't understand that "Hop to it!" was only a figure of speech. A metaphor. Just something people say. So hop to it is what Lulu did, literally. She hopped up on her pile of rocks in the Giant Tire Emporium parking lot and hefted Tiffany Glint's giant tire in the air.

For the rest of his life, Henry never forgot the greedy, gluttonous, disgusting expression of relish on Tiffany Glint's face as she peered into Lulu's eyes while Lulu's imagination slowly shriveled to a speck.

The Firebird crumpled like a used Kleenex. With his very last breath, Henry moaned, "Watch out. I'm *in* the Firebird!" He hardly knew what he was saying.

The *Other* Firebird

Ever so slightly, the pressure crushing Henry eased.

Lulu whispered, "Did you say you were *in* the Firebird?"

"Yes," said Henry blearily, released from the grip of the collapse. "Right here." He drew one more precious breath, the breath he hadn't expected to live long enough to breathe.

"You're sitting in a car," observed Lulu, sounding perplexed.

"Loooloo!" said Tiffany from outside in a threatening voice. "Why the heck is your neck bending like a ballet dancer's? I thought we were done with that hogwash. Especially after the discussion we just had?"

"Just a second, Aunt Tiffany," Lulu gasped. "I'm—trying to think."

"Think?" exclaimed Tiffany. "Think about what? You doubting me again? 'Cause that is what we just agreed you should NOT do!" And then Tiffany fell into a befuddled silence, because she was really wigged out that Lulu hadn't completely caved already under her masterly application of derision.

"Did you meet George Balanchine?" Lulu asked Henry in her imagination, ignoring her aunt. "The world's most famous choreographer?"

Henry said, his mind still a little hazy, "Who's George Balanchine? What's a 'choreographer'? I already told you. I'm Henry Cicada. I'm in the Firebird. I used to polish the hubcaps, and Uncle Leon would give me three dollars each. . . ."

"You *what* the *what*?" said Lulu. "*Who* gave you *how much*?"

"I, um, polished the . . ."

The Firebird radiator sprang a loud, hissing leak.

"Ooooooh," wailed Pim Pom mournfully.

A shelf in the garage holding five hundred pounds of lawn fertilizer collapsed.

Henry knew he was making some kind of mistake. He just didn't know what kind. But it was pretty clear the mention of hubcaps had not gone over well. So he went back one step in the conversation to mention the one thing he knew it was safe to mention. "The Firebird. Whew. Yeah. The Firebird."

"Are we talking about the *Firebird* ballet?" demanded Lulu, her imagination expanding greatly due to the large amount of curiosity she felt about Henry's bizarre mutterings. "Are we talking about the role that catapulted Maria Tallchief, a small-town Oklahoma girl, to international fame?"

"Um," said Henry. "Actually. I was thinking about the *other* Firebird."

"You mean the famous work of art George Balanchine's ballet is *based* on?" gushed Lulu excitedly.

"Yeah!" said Henry. "Right! The one it's *based* on!" All the while, Henry was trying to figure out how in the world a rattly old New Jersey hot rod could possibly lead to a world-famous ballet. Frankly, he hadn't the foggiest. But Henry didn't let that stop him. Being out of ideas never really set Henry Cicada back for very long. "To tell you the truth," Henry said, trying to buy time, "without me, the Firebird would've been pretty dull. You see, I was the one who buffed the car wax to a glossy sheen. . . ."

"I was talking about the famous collaboration between groundbreaking Russian choreographer Michel Fokine and composer Igor Stravinsky," said Lulu, "which in turn inspired the masterpiece by the great George Balanchine. I was not talking about car wax. Wait. A car?" Lulu had a good long look, using her mind's eye, at the automobile parked beside Henry in her mind. "Are you the one who brought that car into my brain?"

"Gee," said Henry, glancing at the pyramid, which stared back at him. "I don't know."

In the meantime, out in the parking lot, Tiffany Glint had gotten over her anger at hearing Lulu ask her to wait, and was now looking for a big stick to hit Lulu in the knee with.

And in her imagination, Lulu figured out what was going on with Henry. What was going on was, Henry Cicada was serving her a great big baloney sandwich. With an extra-large side of hooey. "Henry, you dope," Lulu said. She felt disappointed that an esteemed balletic artist wasn't actually in her brain. She stared off into the distance with a look of disillusionment.

When Tiffany saw that look of disillusionment from outside, she was encouraged and thought maybe Lulu was finally fading back into oblivion, because her eyes were glassy and she wasn't moving. *Maybe*, thought Tiffany, *I've finally got the upper hand on this ding-dong.* So instead of hitting Lulu in the knee with the stick she'd rustled up, Tiffany dropped it and waited to see what would happen next. Tiffany Glint usually tried to avoid hitting people, because, in her experience, there was almost always a better way to inflict pain.

What happened next was, Lulu smiled. Inside her imagination, Henry didn't see Lulu's smile, but he felt it. Like sunshine beaming down on him.

"You know what, Henry?" said Lulu. "If I can't have one of the twentieth century's most important creative geniuses in my brain, like George Balanchine or Igor Stravinsky, then you're a pretty good second choice."

"Thanks, Lulu," Henry said. In the garage of Lulu's imagination, the walls retreated, the Firebird got back into rockin' form, and all the dust settled. The Jaguar reappeared and the green lawn tractor glistened. They were washed, waxed, tuned up, and filled with gas.

"Are you doing OK?" said Lulu. "How's that little dog?"

"We're fine," said Henry.

"Ruff," said Pim Pom.

"I think I get it now, Henry," said Lulu. "That car I keep seeing in my imagination is a Firebird?"

"You got it, Lulu," said Henry. "And it's looking spiffy."

"Interesting," commented Lulu.

Henry decided not to mention that the past few minutes he'd spent inside her mind had almost crushed him to death, suffocated Pim Pom, and triggered near-fatal claustrophobia in both of them, if there was such a thing. Instead, Henry told Lulu, "In fact, just about everything is looking great in your imagination."

"It *feels* good, too," said Lulu.

"Yeah, and by the way," said Henry. "That whole pity privilege thing Tiffany was telling you about? It's definitely bogus. I'm sure the Right On, Raisin! Civic Committee really did spot something inspirational in your dancing."

"Hold on, Henry," said Lulu, boosted by Henry's vote of confidence. "Let me try something. I saw a dance step on PBS the other night. . . ."

On the outside, Tiffany saw Lulu smiling. She saw Lulu arrange her long, graceful limbs in the pose known as first position. And when Tiffany Glint saw that smile, and those arms, legs, and feet, she felt her victory over Lulu evaporating. Which was particularly irksome, because ten minutes before, total annihilation of Lulu MacDougal and whatever preposterous hoo-hah she had pulled to get herself invited onto the Spirit of Raisin float seemed 100 percent assured. Now Tiffany felt like she was back to square one, and she wasn't even sure why. "What the crud is going on?" screeched Tiffany. She glanced around to see where she'd put her stick. Maybe she'd better go ahead and use it on Lulu's knees after all. "What in the Hello Dolly are you fixing to do?" screeched Tiffany.

"I think I'm going to do a little ballet, Aunt Tiffany," replied Lulu.

Tiffany closed her reptile eyes and did her best to focus. Lulu was slipping away from her. She had to do something fast. So she laughed derisively. "By all means, Lulu! Be my guest! 'Cause I am in the mood for some hilarity! I mean—you ain't ever even had a lesson. You just flit around down there in your mom and dad's basement copying off public television shows and YouTube videos. So this oughta be good!"

"Is that true, Lulu? You don't take lessons?" asked Henry.

"I-I'm usually way too shy to dance in front of people," replied Lulu. "Because I really am awfully tall. That day on the parade float, I guess I just got carried away."

Lulu must've said this out loud, because Tiffany guffawed, spit on the ground, and said, "Precisely the concept I've been trying to communicate all evening!"

"But I don't feel too shy anymore," said Lulu. With

that, she executed a perfect tour jeté. Which, if you've ever seen one, is beautiful. And, on top of being beautiful, also distantly resembles a flying backward roundhouse kick.

"Oh yeah?" shouted Tiffany, picking up her stick again and squaring off against Lulu in case she tried another one of those kicks in her direction. "Is that how it's gonna be?"

Meanwhile, in Lulu's imagination, Henry was experiencing a sensation somewhere between riding a roller coaster, swan-diving off a cliff in Acapulco, and performing Bob Beamon's record-setting Mexico City long jump of 1968. "That was fun!" he cried. "Do it again!"

Lulu did it again.

And to Tiffany Glint, standing in front of Lulu brandishing her stick, it somehow looked like maybe Lulu had been tour jeté-ing, um, well, *in her direction*. And this was kind of a problem, because Tiffany Glint, despite her large capacity for evil, was only about four foot eleven, wearing cowboy boots. She weighed, at most, ninety-one pounds. She never engaged in any physical exercise whatsoever. Lulu was, on the other hand, six foot four. And she'd been hoisting a hundred-pound 35X12.50R18 Goodyear All-Terrain steel-belted radial over her head. She had some serious upper-body strength.

And suddenly, despite Tiffany's best efforts, Lulu also

had mental toughness to go with it.

Just for kicks, Lulu prepared a third, completely wicked tour jeté.

Tiffany drew back her stick and took aim at Lulu's right kneecap.

"Lulu, watch out!" cried Henry.

Tiffany swung.

Lulu leaped. There was a sickening crack. Tiffany's stick went flying off across the parking lot in six different directions, shattered by Lulu's graceful but large ballerina foot.

Tiffany ran in fear to her aging all-wheel-drive HumZee Exploder, jumped in, and blew that crazy Tire Emporium in a hail of Texas gravel.

Well, after that, Henry and Lulu hung the "Closed" sign in the door of the Giant Tire Emporium and spent some time in the air-conditioned office, unwinding. Lulu punched four Hyper Colas out of the vending machine by the cash register. She didn't need money, because her aunt Tiffany had jiggered the buttons so it gave away drinks free of charge.

Lulu seated herself in Tiffany's La-Z-Boy recliner, turned the air conditioner to "max," and knocked back a couple of bottles. "Have another Hyper Cola for me!" said Henry from inside Lulu's imagination. So she had a Hyper Cola for Henry. And Henry got it, too, because once you've had a few Hypers, man, those things go straight to your brain, and remember, Lulu's brain was where Henry was. Henry started to feel talkative.

"Lulu," he began. "I have a confession to make."

"What is it, Henry?" asked Lulu.

"I don't really know very much about ballet," said Henry.

"Now there's a shocker," replied Lulu.

"Well, I know ballet is important to you," said Henry, ignoring the good-natured ribbing. At least he hoped it was good-natured. "All the 'choreographics' and 'Ed Balanchine' and so forth."

"*George* Balanchine," said Lulu. "Choreography."

"George Balanchine," said Henry. "I'll read up on it," he promised, "first chance I get."

"That's sweet of you, Henry," said Lulu. "It really is. I mean it."

"The whole time you were talking about a ballet, I was talking about Uncle Leon's righteous set of wheels," admitted Henry. "Funny."

"Hilarious," said Lulu.

Plaster began raining from the ceiling.

"Oh, no," said Henry, ducking. "I thought we were done with that."

"What's happening?" asked Lulu.

"I don't know," answered Henry. A frantic humming emanated from the backseat of the Firebird. When he glanced at the pyramid, it seemed to be scanning some kind of instructions in the distance, like maybe it was getting an update from its mission control or its flight tower or whatever told it what to do. Henry glanced over his shoulder, but saw nothing.

"What's going on?" Henry asked it. The eye widened, in what looked like chagrin. Or possibly embarrassment. Its eyebrow shot up in alarm. "Is there something I should know?" Henry pressed as the oily cement floor buckled, cracked, and disintegrated to reveal a smooth oak floor beneath, much like the floor of a ballet studio. Oak barres began to sprout on the walls. Mirrors appeared and stretched from floor to ceiling. Pim Pom sniffed the air, which drew Henry's attention to the powerful aroma of old pointe shoes.

"What's happening, Henry?" asked Lulu.

"The garage is turning into a ballet studio," said Henry.

"Why?" asked Lulu.

"I don't know," said Henry. "But—" He studied the befuddled look in the pyramid's eye. "Hold on," he said thoughtfully. "Maybe I can guess. *You*—" he said to the pyramid. "*You* got mixed up, too! *You* thought Lulu was imagining a car when she imagined the Firebird, just like I did!"

The pyramid rolled its eye as if to say, *Don't look at me, buddy. I'm doing my best here.* And if pyramids could shrug, this one would've.

"Sure. Of course," mused Henry. "It's all starting to make sense."

"Absolutely," replied Lulu. "Perfect sense!"

Even though he was still getting to know Lulu, Henry got the feeling that when she said, "it makes perfect sense," she actually meant the opposite, so he tried to explain. "When the pyramid and I think of the word 'Firebird,' we think of a classic auto," he said. "So I guess that's why it let me imaginarily bring that imaginary car with me into your imagination when I came. What is it called when people do that?"

He glanced at the pyramid. The pyramid didn't seem to know. "Projection!" Henry remembered. "This is like when people project their own thoughts onto other people's thoughts! See, I had Uncle Leon's ride in my mind already, since whooshing here in the pyramid had just reminded me of whooshing to Atlantic City in his amazing sled. The problem was that to you, 'Firebird' means awesome dancing, but to me, it means motoring sweetness, which is why I made a monkey out of myself! But now that we know you better, I mean the pyramid and me, we know you're imagining ballet when you imagine a Firebird, not a hot rod. Which is probably why my destination, which is also your imagination, now contains a grand piano playing Tchaikovsky on itself."

"Yep, that cleared everything right up," declared Lulu, taking another belt of Hyper Cola. "Although this music is Minkus, not Tchaikovsky."

"Anyway, Lulu," said Henry, thinking now might be a good time to move on to the next subject, "what's the deal with your aunt?"

"I don't know," said Lulu. "She wasn't always like this. When I was little, she took me everywhere with her, and showed me to people, and they told her she had a cute niece. But—she changed."

"Into a raving lunatic," clarified Henry, "when you did ballet on the Spirit of Raisin float and the grand marshal offered you her job."

"Actually, looking back on it now, I feel like there were problems before that," said Lulu thoughtfully.

"Like when?" asked Henry.

"Like when I was nine years old, I told Aunt Tiffany I didn't want to be Aunt Tiffany for Halloween anymore, because I'd been Aunt Tiffany for Halloween since I could walk, and instead I wanted to be Clara Barton, Civil War nurse and founder of the American Red Cross," said Lulu.

"How did that work out?" asked Henry.

"About as well as the Civil War," said Lulu. "Aunt Tiffany blew a fuse, and I ended up being Little Tiffany Glint again."

"Little Tiffany?" repeated Henry.

"Aunt Tiffany went as Grown-up Aunt Tiffany," said Lulu.

"She trick-or-treated with you?" asked Henry. "Disguised as herself?"

"Yes," said Lulu. "And as usual, she kept *all* of the Snickers bars. Hers *and* mine."

"Coldhearted," commented Henry.

"There was also the time I said I didn't want to take baton twirling lessons, because I wanted to go to pottery camp," added Lulu.

"What happened then?" asked Henry.

"While I was away at camp, Tiffany smashed every single pot in her house, and replaced them all with Tupperware," said Lulu. "Mom said not to worry about it, because that's just the kind of thing Tiffany does once in a while, and besides, it actually made her life worse, not mine. But it was still unsettling."

"Wow," said Henry. "You really rub your aunt the wrong way."

"And now, ever since the tour jeté on the parade float," Lulu went on, "things have been getting worse."

"For instance, things like putting you in a Giant Tire Giant costume and making you hold that tire in the air for the whole town to see?" said Henry.

"Yes," replied Lulu. "Things like that. Every time I managed to get my nerve up enough to put the tire down, she said I was stupid to think I could ever be a ballet dancer, since my feet are so big, and I'm as tall as Hagrid, and goofy, and gangling, and gawky, and a whole lot of other words I'm surprised she even knew. And she told me I should be happy because at least there's one thing in the world I'm possibly good for: hoisting tires. And then my mind got all foggy and I couldn't think anymore."

"Why couldn't you ask your mom and dad for help?" wondered Henry.

"They're on an important trip," said Lulu. "And I can only call them in an emergency."

"This wasn't an emergency?" asked Henry.

"Not according to Aunt Tiffany," said Lulu, "who keeps my phone in her purse. I thought about running away. But I couldn't. Because after she did that thing to my brain, I guess I panicked. Everything got hazy. I couldn't imagine how."

"Your Achilles' heel," said Henry thoughtfully.

"My what?" said Lulu.

"Great people always have an overwhelming strength and a calamitous weakness," said Henry. "Achilles had his heel, which was vulnerable to poison arrows. You have your imagination, which is vulnerable to Tiffany Glint."

"I never thought about it like that before, Henry," said Lulu.

"Well, it's a good thing I'm here," observed Henry.

"Are you saying you think I'm great?" asked Lulu.

"You *are* next in line for the Spirit of Raisin," pointed out Henry. "Listen. I was wondering. If Tiffany is so awful, what are you doing hanging around with her in the first place?"

"My mom and dad are the first husband-wife astronaut team in history," said Lulu. "But their astronaut accreditation is about to expire. So they had to go to Houston to renew it. And it's a long process. Aunt Tiffany is taking care of me while they're gone."

"When do they get home?" wondered Henry.

"Tonight," said Lulu.

"So Tiffany isn't going to be in charge of you anymore?" asked Henry.

"Nope," said Lulu.

"Then everything will be fine!" replied Henry.

"I hope so," said Lulu.

"Plus," said Henry, "if your aunt gives you any more trouble, you can just do that awesome move—"

"Tour jeté," supplied Lulu.

"Right," said Henry. "You seem like a really good ballet dancer."

"Thanks, Henry," said Lulu, fiddling with the dial of an old radio that'd been gathering dust in the far corner of the office. A country music guy started singing in a voice as bright as the first day of spring:

> *"Everything's comin' up roses!*
> *I'm the luckiest guy since Moses!"*

Then he plucked out a happy interlude on his plinky guitar and went on:

*"Everything's comin' up roses!
Even when it ain't."*

As Henry listened, he realized that it pretty much summed up how he felt at the moment. Everything *was* coming up roses. Despite about a thousand mysterious and unsettling reasons why it shouldn't be. For a second, his spirits soared as he thought about how much fun it was going to be to tell his dad about all this when he got home, and to have something besides useless Elktonium inventions to talk about at the breakfast table. But almost immediately, he realized the whole story was guaranteed to make his dad sadder than ever, because it was exactly the kind of scenario his mom would've dreamed up: cosmic pyramids, inhabitable imaginations, evil aunts. Well, maybe not the evil aunt part. Tiffany was just way too bizarre for anybody to make up. But the rest of it was definitely Melissa Cicada material.

Also: *if* he ever got home. Because it was far from clear to Henry how that was supposed to happen. This was another challenge he should probably devote some brainpower to before long. . . .

"And that," said the announcer, breaking into Henry's reverie, "was the beloved Lucius Throckmorton, the

Singing Cowboy, with his immortal classic, 'Comin' Up Roses.'"

With an effort, Henry turned his thoughts from Lucius's song back to something Lulu had said a few moments before. "Why do you *hope* things will be OK when your parents get home?" he asked. "How come you're not *sure* things will be OK? Can't your parents take care of you?"

"Of course they can," said Lulu. "But, well, Aunt Tiffany is kinda the *queen* of my hometown."

"I don't know about the Texas you inhabit," said Henry, because he was still not 100 percent sure if he was on Earth or Spudmotron, "but in the one where I live, towns don't have queens. Texas is a democracy."

"I guess she's the *unofficial* queen," said Lulu. "Whatever she is, she runs the whole show. Everybody does what she says all the time. I don't know how she manages it."

"Probably the same way she manages you," mused Henry. "Intimidation and fear."

"Probably," said Lulu.

"Well, when word gets around that she tried to make you into a roadside tire sign," said Henry, "maybe your aunt won't be so popular anymore."

"Or she might just weasel out of trouble like she always does," said Lulu.

"Anyway, you're leaving for college soon, right? So you'll be gone and she won't be able to bother you," said Henry.

Lulu giggled. "I'm in sixth grade."

"Oh," said Henry. "Wow. Same as me. Well, that's OK. I mean, a lot of people get held back. A time or two, even. I mean . . ."

Lulu laughed again. "I didn't get held back. I'm just very tall."

"Sorry," said Henry. "I guess I just assumed—"

"That's all right. People do it all the time. Besides, I should be thanking you," said Lulu. "For helping me."

"Well, I, uh, ah," stammered Henry. "No problem." While he was busy blushing, Henry remembered something. "Hey," he said, "did your aunt ever say anything about *The BFG* by Roald Dahl?"

"Not that I remember," said Lulu. "Why do you ask?"

"She's got a copy in her purse," said Henry.

"Weird," said Lulu. "She's not a big reader."

"I kinda figured," replied Henry.

"You want to go back to my house?" asked Lulu. "I have *The BFG* on my bookshelf. We can try to figure out why Aunt Tiffany is so interested in it. Plus, we could check my mom's science book collection for clues about how you got lodged in my brain."

"Sure," said Henry. "And maybe we can also look for clues about how I'm supposed to get home from here."

That was when Henry noticed the pyramid's eyeball trying to catch his glance. It seemed to be glaring at him. Like it wanted his attention. Like it had a message. An urgent one. The pyramid began to pixelate. "What?" Henry asked it.

"What what?" Lulu asked Henry.

"I was talking to the eyeball on the pyramid," said Henry.

"Right," said Lulu. "While you're at it, tell the eagle holding the arrows Lulu says 'hello.'"

"No, I'm serious," replied Henry. "I'm getting a message in here. I think I'm supposed to get back in the pyramid and go now." The floor of the studio shuddered a bit, as if a minor earthquake had struck, because Lulu suddenly felt anxious at the thought of Henry's leaving, and her imagination flinched. "But I'll come back," said Henry.

"I *hope* you'll come back," said Lulu.

"I will," said Henry. "I promise."

The Elktonium doghouse made its presence known by shimmering more and more fiercely. From its mysterious cosmic mission control headquarters, or wherever its flight plans came from, it was clearly getting the message that its passengers needed to prepare for takeoff.

"Good-bye, Lulu," Henry said. He clambered into the doghouse.

But just before the swoooosh, the strawberry-tangerine light, and the toe-curling acceleration began, Henry heard the radio announcer come on and say, "This just in—local astronaut couple headed for the International Space Station! That's right, our very own Jake and Frieda MacDougal reportedly got word as they were traveling home from Houston that for the next thirteen months, they will be joining the crew of the—"

"Mom? Dad?" Henry heard Lulu cry. "Henry?"

But before they could scramble out of the doghouse, Henry and Pim Pom were speeding through the nothing, and then they were in Henry's backyard.

Maybe, Maybe, Maybe

Henry and Pim Pom staggered out of the dog-house. A rustling came from the shrubberies. Light emanated from the basement windows. They were home.

Henry heard his dad's voice echoing through the ventilator grate. Something about staying away from the pyramid. Well, it was a little late for that.

Henry thought about going down to ask for advice about Lulu, but then he thought better of it, because this was definitely not a topic a guy on a quest to be just plain plain would be wise to bring up.

So Henry tucked Pim Pom under his arm, sneaked inside the house while basement machinery softly whirred, and crept upstairs to his room.

He felt pretty sure he wouldn't be able to fall asleep

that night. Or the next, or the next, or any night for a week, for that matter. He had a lot to think about.

Maybe, he told himself, Lulu was going to be fine. Wherever she was. Maybe Tiffany had been defeated once and for all, and even if her parents were headed for space, and she would be under Tiffany's supervision for the next year and a month, Lulu now had the strength to stand up to her aunt.

Or maybe his interference had only served to rile Tiffany up further and made Lulu's life 100 percent harder, the way he'd made Jurgen's life harder, only more so.

Or maybe, and this seemed most likely, he was going nuts and Lulu didn't exist at all. In which case his quest to be just plain plain was in big trouble. Because crazy people are rarely plain.

Or maybe, or maybe, or maybe . . .

The strange thing was, when he got in bed later, even though he had a million things on his mind, Henry began to drift off almost immediately, Pim Pom curled up in an imaginary hole at his feet.

He didn't yet know about the notes Phil had made that night, but Phil was absolutely correct. A guy with the right doohickey *could* travel all the way to dimensions forty-seven, forty-eight, and forty-nine, and Henry was that guy, because that's how far the doghouse had carried him to get to Lulu's imagination. And traveling through over forty dimensions both ways in a pyramidal Elktonium doghouse while bathed in a strawberry-tangerine light can really knock the zip out of you.

When he woke up the next morning awash in brilliant sunshine, Henry didn't know whether to hope the events of the previous night had been a dream, or to hope that they hadn't. He liked Lulu, and thought it would be nice if she actually existed. On the other hand, *because* he liked Lulu, he hated to think he'd left her without any parents, in the clutches of a demented orange woman who wanted to obliterate her by imploding her mind.

Besides, Henry asked himself, where did all of this fit into his quest to be just plain plain? Henry did a quick calculation and figured there was about a 100 percent chance it didn't.

Sheeesh. What to do?

He climbed out of bed. Jammed in the back pocket of his jeans, which he hadn't bothered to change out of, was a giant ballet slipper. Henry examined it closely. Maybe it had been imaginary at some point in its existence— for instance, when he was in Lulu's imagination. But now the slipper appeared to be perfectly real. Henry rapped it against the wall.

"What?" called his dad from the next room.

"Nothing," replied Henry, stowing the shoe in his sock drawer.

At breakfast, Henry found that Mini-Wheats had never tasted so wheat-y. And orange juice never so tangy. Jelly Jump-Ups had never jumped so high when the freaky little toaster popped. And Elktonium had never looked so beautiful, Henry thought as he gazed at Pim Pom's dog-house through the kitchen window.

Henry felt a feeling he hadn't felt in a while: excitement. Something was happening. Possibly, that something was that he was losing his mind. But something seemed like it might be better than nothing.

"Just remember," Henry reminded himself, "you're on a mission to be plain!" But could he be both, he wondered? At the same time? Excited? And plain? He figured the only way to find out was to try.

Henry's dad sat down at the table with the morning newspaper in his left hand and the scissors in his right as he scanned the headlines to make sure there weren't any so upsetting that he needed to cut them out and hide them from Henry.

Henry decided to skip the clichés that usually passed for conversation at their house, like "Nice morning!" "Great weather!" "How did you sleep?" Or "The dental floss is running short."

"Dad," demanded Henry, "is there anything I should know about Elktonium?"

The question caused Henry's dad to quit hacking at the paper with the scissors (which were made out of Elktonium and were so dull and inept they would've been perfect for the average pre-K Sunday school craft activity because you could basically have stabbed somebody in the eye with them and they'd have done less damage than a soggy Q-tip).

"Elktonium?" said Phil. This was his tactic when he knew the answer to a question Henry had just asked but wasn't sure he wanted to give it: repeat the last word, quizzically.

"Right. Elktonium. The strangely shimmering metal you're always trying to make things out of," prompted Henry. "Created by Mom."

"Mom?" said his dad.

"Mom," confirmed Henry, repeating the repeated word to break the cycle.

"Aha," said his dad, as if it were news to him that

he was constantly making things from Elktonium, which had been created by Melissa. "That." He stared intently out the window for a while.

"Dad?" said Henry.

"I'm trying to think where to start," said his dad.

"How about the beginning?" suggested Henry.

"OK, Henry," agreed his dad. "There's a thing or two you probably should know. I guess the place to start is, your mother wasn't like other scientists."

"No kidding," said Henry.

"She was outrageous. Audacious. Loquacious," said Henry's dad.

"I know," said Henry, "and courageous."

"Not to mention disputatious," said his father, "as well as, occasionally, pugnacious. But that's not entirely pertinent to the question you asked." Henry's father thought for another minute. "Or maybe it is. Anyway, your mother also used to be quite an artist, back when she was in elementary school. She was skilled at pointillism, not to mention decoupage. And of course she was really good at science, too. But after a while, when she got to middle school, her interests started to clash. Science and art, I mean. On standardized tests, she could never decide whether to bubble in the right answers or use the test form to make, you know, a portrait of Abraham Lincoln using the little answer ovals."

"Yeah," said Henry. Because he had the same problem. Well, he wasn't as advanced as his mother had been. He'd never attempted a presidential portrait. But he'd been known to bubble in his share of Christmas trees and right and left arrows on the Scantron forms for statewide competency exams. Back when just plain plainness was the last thing on his mind.

"So anyway, she was enough of a brainiac to hold it all together up to her senior year of high school, but then everything boiled down to a choice she had to make when it came to college," continued Henry's dad. "Because she was offered a Melman scholarship."

"Wow," said Henry. "A Melman scholarship!"

"Yes!" said his dad.

"What's a Melman scholarship?" asked Henry.

"Only a few people a year are awarded Melman scholarships," explained Henry's dad. "The three most promising young artists in the country. Your mother turned it down."

"Why?" said Henry. Something about this conversation felt strange to him.

"Because she was also offered a Halbfunt fellowship."

"Wow!" said Henry. "A Halbfunt!" Then, after a couple of seconds, he asked, "What's that?"

"They only offer *two* of those," said Henry's dad proudly. "To the most gifted young scientists in the country."

"So she decided to become a scientist," mused Henry. Yes. The conversation *did* feel strange to Henry. But not because it was strange. Not because it was about decoupage, pointillism, and the Halbfunt fellowship all at once. No, Henry's conversation with his father felt strange because, for once, it didn't feel sad.

"Yes," his dad was saying. "But your mom still had that artistic streak, you know. So when she went to college, she'd bombard atoms in the lab all morning, and paint an abstract-expressionist trompe l'oeil after lunch. Now, Henry, there are certain critics and cobweb-brained professors who will try to tell you an abstract-expressionist trompe l'oeil is an artistic, aesthetic, and theoretical impossibility. But none of us work-study students in the reference section of the library cared. We really admired your mom's abilities."

Henry had never known about his mother's art, but now that he was hearing about it, he liked how it sounded.

"She had this idea once for a really interesting piece

of performance art," continued his dad. "You know what performance art is, right?"

"Art in which the actions of an individual or a group in a particular place and time constitute the work?" said Henry.

"Right on," said his dad. "Anyway, your mom made a Teleological Telephone Booth—"

"What's that?" asked Henry.

"Teleology?" asked his dad.

"No. What's a telephone booth?" said Henry.

"Long ago," said his dad, "people didn't have iPhones and πPhones and skyPhones and Robots to carry around in their pockets. So when they had to make a telephone call, there were these little glass houses with an old-fashioned pay telephone inside that you could use for ten cents."

"Amazing," said Henry.

"And 'teleology' is the attempt to find the meaning of life," added his dad.

"That's cool, too," said Henry. "So what did the Teleological Telephone Booth do?"

"When people took part in the performance," said Henry's dad, "she gave each one a dime, which they dropped into the pay phone. And then they could hear just about anything."

"Like a German shepherd can hear just about anything?" asked Henry.

"No," said his dad. "Like just about *anything*. That ever happened. When I got my turn to sit on the shiny stool and lift the glowing receiver connected to the luminous telephone, I heard Ludwig van Beethoven dreaming up Symphony Number Seven. I put in another dime and heard Charles Dickens think of the name for a brand-new character: David Copperfield. Then I put in my last dime and I heard Emily Dickinson decide that hope is the thing with feathers."

"Like you heard their brain waves?" asked Henry.

"Like that," said his dad.

"You'd think waves from Ludwig van Beethoven's brain would be long gone by now," mused Henry.

"You would," said Phil. "But Melissa's work of art conveyed a message."

"What was the message?" asked Henry.

"We're all here," said Phil.

"I don't get it," said Henry.

"I didn't, either," said his dad, "but that's what the sign on the door of the phone booth said: 'We're all here.'"

"Wow," said Henry. "Outrageous."

"Courageous," said his father.

"'We're all here,'" echoed Henry. "Audacious."

"It certainly was," said his father, sounding down-hearted, and now Henry didn't think the conversation felt strange at all. In fact, it was moving into familiar territory: sadness. But he couldn't stop. He needed to know more.

"How did she do it?" asked Henry. "How did she play what was in Charles Dickens's imagination?

"Don't know," said his dad. "*She* was the creative genius. After she was gone, I once tried to look the Teleological Telephone Booth up in her notes. I always *could* look things up," he added, sounding melancholy.

"You always *could* look things up, Dad," affirmed Henry. "When it comes to looking things up, nobody can touch you."

"Thanks," said Henry's dad. "But in reference to the Teleological Telephone Booth, all I found was one yellowish file card pinned to the bulletin board on the door of her lab. It said something about remembering to connect the TTB to the Scheme of Things. But I don't actually know what that means, or if she ever got around to doing it."

Henry's dad fell silent. Henry's thoughts returned to

the words his mom had inscribed on her creation. "We're all here," he said quietly.

"So anyway, Henry," his dad began again briskly, "even after she got over her artistic phase, your mom was still pretty creative, for a scientist, and one thing she really enjoyed was rearranging subatomic particles. You know, moving electrons, which circle around the nucleus of the atom, from orbit to orbit." For a moment, Phil became lost in thought, remembering his brilliant wife. "Say, Henry, did you know that when you move the electrons of certain atoms, you can make a machine that thinks?"

"Sheesh, Dad," said Henry. "I know how computers work."

"Well," Phil said. "Like many people nowadays, your mother knew how to leave little messages embedded in certain arrangements of atoms. Like scientists long ago learned how to do with computers, using atoms of the well-known element silicon, which is common sand."

"Dad!" said Henry. "I know! I know that silicon is nothing more than common sand!"

"Sorry," said Phil.

"Stop trying to explain computers to me!" said Henry.

"I said I was sorry," said his dad.

"Why are you telling me all this?" wondered Henry.

"What does it have to do with Elktonium?"

"Well, see," said Henry's dad, "your mother's interest wasn't just limited to silicon. In the past twenty-four hours, I have found evidence that possibly she could've had something spectacular in mind for the new metal, Elktonium! To send messages. To store information. You know—put this gaggle of particles here, it means two plus two equals four, put that gaggle there, it means return the library books, take these four hundred billion billion billion subatomic entities and move them forty-nine whole dimensions, and well, maybe you start solving the mysteries of human existence!"

"That might've been useful," allowed Henry.

"Possibly," said Phil. "I believe your mother was trying to arrange all the atomic particles into just the right shape, into something like, um"—he glanced through the back window for an example—"that doghouse out there." He pointed to Pim Pom's pyramidal new home. "I believe she envisioned a thinking machine more powerful than all the computers in history put together. Something like a human mind, with powers maybe even greater. If she could've arranged the crystal structure just right. If she could've activated it with the perfect level of energy, with maybe, I don't know, a burst of light that was exactly the right color—that is to say, wavelength. . . ."

"I *know* that the wavelength of light determines its color, Dad," said Henry. But his dad didn't hear. He was gazing at the Elktonium doghouse in the backyard, lost in thought.

"At least," Phil said wistfully, "Melissa had a chance to give Elktonium that nifty iridescent green color. How far she got with the rest of her vision, I really don't know." And now he sounded very sad.

And it was on the tip of Henry's tongue to spill the beans to his dad, to tell him that Elktonium definitely had capabilities somebody needed to check into, and to fill him in on the Firebird and Lulu and Tiffany Glint, to ask for advice, to compare notes, to converse, discuss, confabulate, and to get help figuring out what was real and what wasn't. But his dad was already sad enough without having to listen to outrageousness guaranteed to remind him of Melissa, Henry figured.

"Maybe I better get to work inventing something useful out of Elktonium," said his dad, ending the conversation the way he ended almost all their conversations.

"OK, Dad," said Henry. "Bye."

Phil headed downstairs with an untoasted Jelly Jump-Up in each hand.

A cloud passed overhead, darkening the backyard and the Elktonium pyramid. Henry's eye fell on the newspaper his dad had left behind. Underneath a story about paramilitary forces in Africa, which his dad had been gnawing at with the Elktonium scissors, Henry saw an article that froze his blood: "Husband and Wife Astronaut Team Prepare to Blast Off!" And there they were. Jake and Frieda MacDougal, smiling for the cameras, in their space suits, proud and happy to be called into service for a top-secret last-minute emergency mission to the International Space Station.

Their only daughter, Lulu, according to the article, was very proud of them. So was Frieda's older sister, Tiffany.

This could only mean one thing: Lulu was real!

And therefore—so was Tiffany. And so was Lulu's awful predicament.

Henry sprinted into the yard. Pim Pom followed at his heels, yipping in alarm. The cloud had passed and the sun blazed yellow overhead. The doghouse looked sort of green-y, maybe a little shiny around the edges, but not the same magical, shimmering, iridescent color as last night. Something seemed different from before, not quite cosmic. Not quite right. Henry halted. He glanced around the yard, looking for something to toss into the doghouse to see if it was working before he jumped in. Eventually, he spotted somebody's old iron-handled golf club in the gnarled creosote-bush shrubbery, and chucked it into the doghouse, hoping to see it disappear in a blinding flash. But all the old golf club did was clank around on the floor and lie there. His heart sinking, Henry climbed inside the house. But it was as he feared. Nothing. No hot-rod–like acceleration, no strawberry-tangerine light, no Lulu.

All Henry could do was lie on the floor of Pim Pom's house and stare gloomily at the ceiling, clutching the golf club against his chest.

"Ahem," Henry heard from somewhere outside. "Aherrm!"

A Voice from the Shrubberies

Henry stuck his head out the door. "Ahhhhhh-ha-ha-ha-herrrrrrrm," he heard again. His backyard appeared unchanged. The sky, the trees, the house on Bill Street, the shrubs. Suddenly, a short stubby man who looked like he might be part walrus burst from the hedge. Or—and this was somewhat less plausible—a short stubby walrus who looked like he might be part man burst from the hedge.

"Young fellow," said the person or walrus (although since it was speaking, person was looking more and more like the verdict), "kindly return my mashie." Henry crawled dejectedly out of the doghouse. Pim Pom followed with droopy ears.

"I *would* return your mashie," said Henry, "if I knew what a 'mashie' was."

The man twirled his bushy side-whiskers, rearranging them into a truly walrus-like configuration, and said, "Have you anything that doesn't belong to you? Anything at all that might belong to someone else? Perhaps, for instance, to me? Have you anything that might conceivably be my mashie niblick?"

Henry glanced inside the doghouse. "Well," he said. "I've got this old golf club." And he retrieved it.

"Brilliant!" said the man with whiskers. "My old iron mashie. Some people refer to it as a 'sand wedge.' Hand it over." Henry did. "Now," said the man, "explain yourself."

"I wasn't trying to steal your mushy," said Henry.

"Mashie!" said the man.

"Mashie!" said Henry. "Sorry. I just found it lying in the stinky desert shrubberies," said Henry, "over near the neighbor's yard, and I picked it up."

"The shrubberies are not stinky," said the man. "They smell of creosote, a remarkable chemical which protects them from drought, and which can be extracted and used to preserve telephone poles and railroad crossties, or to treat painful skin conditions."

"Oh," said Henry. "I didn't know these bushes all over the place in the desert were remarkable." He had a closer look at them. Kinda interesting, sure.

"By the way, have you *met* your neighbor?" asked the man.

"General G. G. P. Hedgerow?" said Henry, recalling the strange name from the next-door mailbox.

"Yes," said the man, "General G. G. P. Hedgerow!"

"No, I haven't," said Henry.

"There's where you're wrong!" roared the man. Henry blinked in surprise. "Because *I* am your neighbor! General Galahad G. P. Hedgerow, Royal British Marines, retired. And you have now met me." He stuck out his hand. Henry took it.

"Henry Cicada," said Henry. "Pleased to meet you, General." And, to his surprise, he really was. Something about the general, he liked. He just wasn't quite sure what.

"Cicada," said General Hedgerow. "Unusual name." Henry didn't mention to the general that you don't exactly see "Hedgerow" painted on a mailbox every day.

"You were explaining?" said General Hedgerow.

"I was just testing the doghouse with your golf club," said Henry.

"Oh, I see," said General Hedgerow. "Perfectly clear to me now."

Henry examined General Hedgerow closely to see if he were joking. It was impossible to tell. General Hedgerow, being British, hadn't changed his facial expression in thirty-seven years.

"Come look at this!" ordered General Hedgerow, pointing through the shrubberies toward his house. "It might buck you up!"

"I don't need bucking up," said Henry. He didn't exactly know what bucking up was. All he could think of was Lulu, left alone in Raisin with her horrible aunt.

"You'll like it," said the general, making his way through the bushes. "Young fellows always do. Makes them quite cheerful, you know, quite cheerful."

"Is 'bucked up' the same thing as 'cheerful'?" asked Henry.

"Indubitably," answered the general faintly from the yard next door, where he had wandered. "Nothing like a motor scooter to buck up a glum little nipper like yourself."

"How did you know I needed bucking up?" said Henry, trailing along. "Is it *that* obvious?"

In reply, General Hedgerow broke with thirty-seven years' worth of tradition and raised one ironical eyebrow. Then he turned and marched purposefully around the front of his house, which, from certain angles, looked a little haunted. Cobwebs in the doorway, drearily drooping trees, black cat on the porch, all that. Henry followed the general, not too concerned about the haunted aspect of the house. But maybe a little concerned. As soon as General Hedgerow got to the edge of his driveway, he hopped three feet, came down on his toes, scooted two steps to the right, and zigzagged nine feet due northwest until he arrived next to a tarpaulin-shrouded object in front of the garage. Henry watched in amazement. For an old fellow, General Hedgerow was pretty light on his feet. "Step exactly where I stepped," said General Hedgerow. "Otherwise—the man-traps."

"Man-traps?" said Henry.

"Did I stutter?" asked the general.

Henry didn't really think the general was expecting an answer to this question, so he took a deep breath and crossed the driveway just like he'd seen General Hedgerow do. Hopped three feet. Came down on his toes. Scooted two steps to the right, and zigzagged nine feet due northwest. He made it to the tarpaulin-shrouded shape unscathed. "Excellent," beamed General Hedgerow. He swept the tarpaulin off the object, which was obviously fabulously valuable, since it was guarded by man-traps capable of—

"OK, now will you tell me what man-traps actually

do?" requested Henry.

"Trap men," said the general, "in rather . . . unpleasant ways."

Henry got the impression that "unpleasant" was a *kind* way to describe what man-traps did.

"Look!" the general said.

"A scooter," said Henry.

"A 1942 Muckeridge-Pressley," said General Hedgerow.

"Wow," said Henry, because he had to admit, on closer inspection, the little machine was something to behold. Like a bullet, painted orange, with handlebars. "How fast will it go?" he asked, noticing that the Muckeridge-Pressley also seemed to come equipped with a sidecar shaped like a small zeppelin.

"Got a motor capable of .9 horsepower!" said General Hedgerow proudly. "So—thirty-three and one-third miles per hour. Downhill. With a stiff tailwind."

"Oh," said Henry, a little disappointed. "I can just about pedal my bike that fast. Downhill. With a tailwind."

"Sometimes, in an emergency, there are techniques for making the Muckeridge-Pressley go a little faster," allowed General Hedgerow.

"How much faster?" asked Henry.

"That's a proprietary secret of the Queen of England," said General Hedgerow, "who was once my boss."

Now this sounded promising.

"What's that big clamp on the zeppelin-shaped side-car?" asked Henry.

"It's the jig for the auxiliary rocket motor," said General Hedgerow.

"The auxiliary rocket motor," said Henry thoughtfully, making a mental note to come back to that one later. "Where could somebody go on the Muckeridge-Pressley?" he asked.

"Just about anywhere somebody could imagine," replied the general.

Henry got a faraway look in his eye as he imagined destinations. Raisin. Houston. Philadelphia. If life ever got more cheerful, maybe Disneyland would be fun to visit?

"Right-o," said the general, studying Henry's expression closely, "despite your difficult circumstances, your imagination seems to be in working order. Very good news, that. Because when those blighters collapse, you can end up Nowhere."

"What?" asked Henry in alarm, but the rumble of the

approaching school bus drowned out his question. "People whose imaginations collapse are headed—"

"Nowhere," supplied the general for a second time, "in certain cases."

"The same Nowhere as in 'just this side of Nowhere'?" asked Henry.

"The very one," replied General Hedgerow.

"Is that a place people can actually go?" asked Henry.

"Certainly," said the general. "If said people have transportation. Although when they arrive, these people run the distinct risk of becoming Nowhere Men—or Women—making plans for nobody."

"Could you show me how to ride the Muckeridge-Pressley?" Henry asked. "I mean," he added hastily, "just around the neighborhood?"

General Hedgerow scratched his head. Then he scratched his chin whiskers. After that, he scratched something inside his infantry boot. He cleared his throat, took a deep breath, let the breath out, paced a bit, and sighed.

General Hedgerow sat down, and he stood up.

General Hedgerow laid his index finger against his nose and closed one eye. He studied the Muckeridge-Pressley, and then he studied Henry.

Then General Hedgerow closed his other eye, but

only after having opened the first eye, because if General Hedgerow had learned anything in the Royal Marines, it's that you don't go standing around in broad daylight with both eyes closed.

"Certainly, m'boy," said General Hedgerow finally. "Right after school."

"What about now?" asked Henry.

The school bus stopped a block away.

"You must attend to your lessons. I understand it is the law in these parts," replied the general. "Stop by afterward. I'll give you a tutorial on the old M-P. Far safer than traveling by pyramid, and much less likely to land you in unfamiliar territory."

"Wait! What? How do you know about the pyramid?" asked Henry.

But the general was already shutting his front door behind him.

The school bus rounded the corner.

Henry scooped up Pim Pom, ran to his yard, set him inside the door of 339 Bill Street, grabbed his backpack, and waited patiently while his puppy licked him good-bye. He wondered how the general could possibly know about Pim Pom's pyramid and how he made the word "Nowhere" sound capitalized.

Maria Tallchief

Meanwhile, back in Raisin, Texas, Earth, solar system, Milky Way, when Lulu came down to breakfast, she was a little surprised to find Tiffany Glint sitting at her mother's kitchen table bawling, since the last time she'd seen Tiffany, Tiffany had been fleeing down Highway 99999 in a dented HumZee. "I'm so sorry, Lulu," wailed Tiffany. "I'm so sorry about what I did. I don't know what came over me."

Lulu noticed that under her chair, Tiffany had her pointy boots aimed at the back door.

"You gonna lunge at me?" asked Tiffany, eyeing Lulu cautiously.

"No, Aunt Tiffany," replied Lulu.

"I just want to be friends, honey," said Tiffany. "I let myself in with the spare key just to tell you I want things to go back to the way they were. Before the whole Tire Giant thing. And the Spirit of Raisin thing. I want things to be like when you were a tiny little cute bugbear that wore the red cowboy boots just like mine that I bought you."

"I remember the red cowboy boots," replied Lulu carefully. She didn't know what to make of her aunt's change of heart. And as for those boots, actually, Lulu MacDougal was one of only three native-born Texans known to despise cowboy boots. She especially despised red ones. But she'd always told herself that Tiffany was only trying to be nice when she gave that gift, so she should appreciate them. "Thanks," Lulu added.

"Oh, please! Oh, please!" wailed Tiffany. "I'm sorry. I know I'm a bad woman. I see that now. And now that I see that, I guaran-dang-tee, my bad behavior is over."

"It is?" asked Lulu, picking out a peach from the fruit bowl for breakfast. She couldn't keep from hoping this was true. She couldn't resist the temptation to believe that she and her aunt really would be able to get along, like in the old days, when she could barely talk. Lulu missed those days.

Also, her parents were going to be absent from the planet for the next thirteen months, making Tiffany her closest relative on Earth.

"Yeah!" said Tiffany, carefully resealing the box of doughnut holes she'd been scarfing. "Sure. Bad behavior over. See, my problem was, I didn't have the advantages in life. I didn't have the opportunities. I didn't have the prospects. I missed all the breaks. And I therefore became a terrible person. A bad woman. I see that now. And it's all because of you, Lulu. That I see I'm terrible. Aww, I'm no good at putting these things into words. Let's just say you have showed me the terror of my ways! Thank you! Thank you!"

"Error of your ways," said Lulu.

"Error, whatever," said Tiffany. "Much appreciated! I mean it!"

"You're welcome," said Lulu.

Tiffany blinked at her. "Now get in my new car," she said, standing up from the table.

"Why, Aunt Tiffany?" asked Lulu.

"Because if your parents are going to be in space for thirteen months like they told me they are, and I'm gonna be in charge of you the whole time like they asked me to be, then we are gonna be friends, and I am gonna make sure to take real good care of you that whole time," said Tiffany. "So now get in my car so I can drive you to school."

"Are you sure they asked you?" wondered Lulu. "To take care of me the whole time? I mean, have you got a signed request? Because maybe, I just thought of this, I could stay at my neighbors' house part of the time, if we need a, um, break from each other?"

"Your parents telephoned," said Tiffany sullenly. "And asked. So I don't got a note."

"Could they, I don't know, email a secure document?" asked Lulu.

"WHY DON'T YOU BELIEVE ME? WHY *WOULDN'T* THEY ASK ME?" screeched Tiffany. "I'm your mother's favorite sister. Plus, I'm her only sister. Plus, there's nobody else to ask. I am specifically what you get! Now go outside and get in the car."

Lulu went outside with her and climbed into the car. It was a long way up, even for her. Tiffany had to use a stepladder, which the HumZee salesman had thrown in as a bonus when she bought the silly vehicle.

By the time Tiffany reached the end of Lulu's street in her new HumZee, she was doing seventy-seven, which was actually considered too fast for a residential area, even in Raisin. But it hurt Tiffany's car to go slow. Seventy-seven was about the minimum she could run it.

The fact was, Tiffany's brand-new sled was a honkin' HumZee Exploder, equipped with not one but *four* V-8 engines, one for each wheel. (Let's see, four times eight, that's V-32. A lot!) It was painted the brightest color of any vehicle in automotive history, Plutonium Pink. It was bigger than a HumVee. Bigger than a HumDouble-U. Bigger than a HumEX. Even bigger than a HumWhy. It was the biggest vehicle on record. The HumZee was so big, in fact, that if it ever accidentally ran into another, reasonably sized car, that unfortunate car would instantly explode into a misty cloud of metallic confetti, due to the HumZee's immense size. Hence the name: Exploder.

Tiffany's HumZee Exploder was forty-one feet long, weighed thirteen tons, and used three gallons of gas to go nineteen feet. The HumZee Exploder is a *mighty* popular SUV with people like Tiffany Glint. And the best part was, it was *very* expensive! $49,999. Tiffany left the price sticker in the window, just to make sure nobody lost sight of this fact.

And where had Tiffany Glint gotten $49,999? That was almost exactly how much money Lulu's mom and dad had wired to her bank account to pay for groceries, books, toothpaste, and emergencies while they were away at the International Space Station. And yesterday evening when Tiffany had seen the Plutonium Pink Exploder in the lot, well, *that* was an emergency, wasn't it? Because what if somebody else bought it before she did?

Almost best of all, this particular HumZee model came with a kayak strapped to the luggage rack. Tiffany had no intention of ever paddling a kayak, especially since she lived in the desert, but she thought having it up there made her look competent, in an outdoorsy way.

"Ummm," Tiffany said as she sawed the wheel back and forth, navigating neighborhood corners at high speed. Then she fell quiet. Then she exhaled noisily. Then she said, "My, oh, my."

Lulu tried to ignore all this.

"Boy, howdy," sighed Tiffany Glint. "Man alive. Phew. Well . . ."

Lulu did her best to pay no heed to her aunt's wistful noises. She really did.

"HOOOOOOOOOOOOOOOOO!" exhaled Tiffany.

"What is it, Aunt Tiffany?" said Lulu finally.

"Glad you asked!" said Tiffany Glint. "For I did some thinking last night, when I was parked in my HumZee alone with my thoughts beneath the desert sky, before your mom called, with nothing to contemplate but my own morality, after you tried to kick my head in."

"Do you mean 'mortality'?" asked Lulu. Usually, as she knew from books, when people are alone beneath the desert sky, they contemplate their own "mortality," which means they think about whether their lives have any meaning. "And I didn't try to kick your head in. I was just doing a tour jeté."

"Um," said Tiffany Glint. "Yeah. Mortality. That was it. Also I'm glad to hear you weren't trying to kick my head in."

"I was only dancing," confirmed Lulu.

"Hummmph," said Tiffany darkly. "Dancing. Anyway, like I said, I'm real sorry. And what I'm sorry about is, I'm sorry *you* misunderstood what *I* was trying to accomplish on your behalf. I'm sorry *you* are so ungrateful when somebody is just looking out for you, like *I* was doing. I'm sorry *you* don't recognize a true attempt to help you when you see it, like preparing you to be the Giant Tire Giant, which is a more appropriate role for you, in *my* opinion. But whatevs."

"There's my school," said Lulu, pointing to the large brick building a block away.

"Hey, let's have a fun conversation," suggested Tiffany without hearing or lifting the gas pedal off the floor. "Why don't you tell me something important to you, like, who is your favorite ballerina?"

"Maria Tallchief," replied Lulu, forgetting about school in her enthusiasm for this famous dancer.

"Nice," said Tiffany distractedly, turning left onto the highway that led out of town and cutting off an oncoming school bus in the process. "Marcia Skywalker. What did she do?"

"Maria Tallchief!" corrected Lulu.

"Right," said Tiffany. "Maria Tallchief. That's who I'm talking about."

"Maria Tallchief," said Lulu excitedly, "was America's first prima ballerina. She was born in Fairfax, Oklahoma, and her Osage family name was Ki He Kah Stah Tsa. She started lessons when she was three. When she was eight, she moved to Los Angeles, and when she was seventeen, she moved to New York City. She joined the Ballet Russe de Monte Carlo, where she met the famous choreographer George Balanchine. When Balanchine founded the future New York City Ballet in 1946, Maria became its first star. Balanchine's inspired choreography and Maria's passionate dancing revolutionized the ballet world. Maria's work in *The Firebird* lifted her to the heights of the dance world, and her Sugarplum Fairy made *The Nutcracker* the most popular ballet in history."

"And you like her why?" asked Tiffany.

"I like her," said Lulu, "because she's Maria!"

"That sounds about par for the course," muttered Tiffany.

"What, Aunt Tiffany?" asked Lulu.

"That was a wonderful story!" warbled Tiffany.

"Aunt Tiffany," said Lulu, pointing out the rear window. "You drove right past my school."

"About that," said Tiffany. "As your duly appointed guardian while your parents are in space, I called your principal this morning. To say you weren't coming."

"Why?" asked Lulu.

"'Cause Lulu, it's time to put you on the road," replied Tiffany.

"What road, Aunt Tiffany?" asked Lulu.

"The road to being the next Maria Tallchief!" cried Tiffany, punching her HumZee to ninety as she hit the outskirts of town.

Wild Kingdom

Back on Bill Street, Henry didn't manage to catch the bus after all, because he thought it would be rude to run off before Pim Pom finished licking his face good-bye, and Pim Pom was turning out to be an enthusiastic face licker, so Henry ended up walking to school, which at least got him out of having to deal with Theotis, Jurgen, the gaggle of kids, Shirley Tantrum, and the guy setting up traffic cones. It wasn't that Henry didn't like Jurgen, the gaggle of kids, or the guy setting up traffic cones (though sadly, the same could not be said for Theotis and Shirley). It was just that his list of worries had gotten so long that he couldn't devote any time to these people today.

Henry managed to get through two hours of school without incident. But then, seventeen minutes into band rehearsal, sitting in the fourteenth trumpet chair with his Phillies cap pulled low, puzzling over everything the general had said that morning and trying to appear just plain plain, he realized his part in "When the Saints Go Marching In" was fast approaching.

Henry glanced around to make an inventory of all the people he was about to embarrass himself in front of. Jurgen sat in the trombone section, staring at the ceiling, which guaranteed that he wouldn't make eye contact with anybody, especially not Theotis T. Otis the Third, who stood in the back wielding the kettledrum mallet like a hammer.

Shirley perched smugly in the flutes' first chair, surfing Italian shoes on her iPhone.

Mr. Maurice Graveltrain, the band director, waved his fiberglass baton enthusiastically in the air.

They were about to learn, Henry reflected, that he was the worst trumpet player in Pumpjack, Texas.

There were two reasons for Henry's atrociousness:

One, Henry's trumpet was made of Elktonium, and along with all of Elktonium's other drawbacks, it was just about as resonant as a soggy pup tent.

Two, Henry was a terrible trumpet player.

Here came Henry's notes on the music in front of him.

He took a deep breath, closed his eyes, and blew for all he was worth. A series of wet farting noises emerged from his horn. The rest of the band fell silent, in awe of the sheer terribleness of Henry's playing. Mr. Graveltrain looked at Henry with horror, pity, and panic in his eyes. The band room echoed with the sound of Henry's Elktonium-enhanced Dixieland flatulence.

Even Theotis T. Otis the Third dropped his kettle-drum mallet in disgust. "Dang, dropped my hammer," said Theotis.

"It's not a hammer, Theotis," said Mr. Graveltrain. "It's a *mallet*."

"Fine, whatever," said Theotis. "The important thing is, you hit stuff with it."

After Theotis had stuck his mallet, or hammer, or whatever, in his back pocket, Mr. Graveltrain regretfully turned his attention back to Henry. "Oh, little brother," said Mr. Graveltrain gently (all in all, he was a good-hearted man). "That's just not right."

Henry put his horn down. Mr. Graveltrain looked at him. The entire clarinet section looked at him. All the flute players looked at him. The tuba player looked at him. Every single drummer looked at him. Even Theotis T. Otis the Third looked at him. And it wouldn't have been so bad if they'd looked at him with expressions of amusement, mockery, or even distaste. It would've been better, Henry thought as he sat squirming in fourteenth chair, if every single member of the band had howled with derision. Because what was happening to him at that moment was worse. Everybody in the band was shooting him glances of—sympathy. They all felt sorry for him. Because he was such a bad trumpet player.

The Philadelphia Phillies cap his dad had gotten permission from the school psychologist for him to wear on his still-bald head inside the building probably wasn't helping. People must think Henry had some awful disease, he knew. When really, all he had was an overwhelming desire to achieve plainness.

Finally, Mr. Graveltrain broke the silence and said, "Listen. How important is this to you, Hepcat? I mean, is music something you really want to do, Daddy-O? Because, Slick, I gotta tell ya . . ."

And Henry wanted to shout, "Listen, if my mother hadn't come up with this crazy metal and neglected to endow it with any useful properties because she was so sick, and if my dad hadn't gotten himself fired from his job for spending all his time inventing things like this poor sad Elktonium horn in her honor, I'd be out of band like a shot, but I can't quit band, because my mom *did* create Elktonium and my dad *did* make a horn out of it and he *did* give it to me and I love them both so I've got to stay in this room with you and play this stupid trumpet."

But Henry didn't say this stuff. And even if he had, it wouldn't have made a whole lot of sense to anybody, not even to him. So he just sat there staring at unfortunate Mr. Graveltrain. *Well*, Henry thought as the silence dragged on. *At least things can't get much worse.*

Whereupon a peppy woman appeared in the doorway of the band room and things got worse. "Henry Cicada?" she called. "Would you come with me?"

As Henry got busy packing up his trumpet, Mr. Graveltrain said, "Thank you, School Psychologist Skandar." Try as he might, Mr. Graveltrain couldn't hide the relief he felt that Henry was leaving his band room, at least for a little while.

Theotis stood behind his kettledrums, smacking his hammer, that is to say, mallet, into his meaty fist, watching darkly as Henry exited.

As School Psychologist Skandar closed the door of her office, she smiled and said, "Henry, I'm School Psychologist Skandar."

"I'm Henry Cicada," said Henry as he tried to get comfortable in the chair School Psychologist Skandar offered him. (There was no way to get comfortable in the chair. School Psychologist Skandar had ordered it from a special supply outlet for school psychologists who believe that uncomfortable chairs lead to faster results.)

"I know who you are, Henry," she replied pleasantly. "I'm the one who approved the hat-wearing form your father submitted." School Psychologist Skandar was pretty. Very pretty. She looked sort of like a movie star, a movie star who wore weight-lifting shoes and displayed one gold tooth with the state of Texas engraved on it. That gold tooth actually put a big dent in School Psychologist Skandar's otherwise glamorous looks, in Henry's opinion. Maybe she'd gotten it, Henry thought, so people would forget about her looks and take her seriously.

"Before we begin, is there anything *you* want to talk about?" asked School Psychologist Skandar. Henry ran through his list silently and wondered if it would be worthwhile mentioning her tooth.

"No," he replied. School Psychologist Skandar chucked him good-naturedly on the shoulder. Ouch. Henry rubbed it. School Psychologist Skandar was a member of a workout club that required her to roll a five-hundred-pound tractor tire around an abandoned airplane hangar every day at lunch.

"Are you sure, Henry?" she persisted.

"Well," said Henry. "I do kind of have a question that maybe a psychologist would know the answer to. I mean, you understand about the human mind and everything, right?" said Henry.

"It's my specialty," she said.

"Well, OK," said Henry. "What happens when somebody's imagination collapses?"

School Psychologist Skandar looked alarmed. "Why?" she asked. "Do you feel like your imagination is collapsing?"

"No," said Henry. "But I think it may be happening to a, um, friend."

"Oh. A *friend*. OK," she said, eyeing Henry carefully, "then I'll tell you. When your imagination collapses, I mean completely collapses, so there's not even room in there for one of those scrunchie hair bands the girls wear in PE class, then you're done for. Kaput. Kaplooie. You're doomed. Your life's not worth living. Can't be fixed."

"Could it land you in, um, someplace called—Nowhere?" blurted out Henry. He tried to make it sound capitalized, like the general had done.

"Nowhere," said the psychologist severely, "crosses the line. Nowhere is not something I'm certified to talk about. I have to be even more certified than I already am"—she waved at a wall covered with certificates—"to talk about Nowhere." She frowned and jotted notes furiously in a yellow binder. Then, as she looked up at Henry, she arranged her face in a smile. "But, off the record, do you think one of your friends is headed toward Nowhere? Or—are you?"

"No, no, no," backtracked Henry quickly. "Absolutely not. Nowhere is just something I—heard about." He realized he'd never be able to help Lulu if School Psychologist Skandar got concerned and put him in some kind of special after-school program for doomed kids with collapsing imaginations whose lives were not worth living and were potentially headed for Nowhere. "But thanks for filling me in."

"You're welcome," School Psychologist Skandar said. "Now, listen, Henry. There's something I need to talk to you about."

"Yes, ma'am?" said Henry, the way he'd heard these other Texas kids do.

"I know what's up—" she said.

"Really?" interrupted Henry, because it was hard to

believe that School Psychologist Skandar, even though she seemed pretty smart, knew what was "up." Elktonium, collapsing garages, evil aunts, and wayward toasters? Come on! No way.

"—with Jurgen and Theotis."

"Oh," said Henry. "OK." If you left out every aspect of his life apart from Jurgen and Theotis, which was leaving out a lot, then OK. It seemed plausible that maybe, just maybe, she knew what was up with them.

"When I was a kid," School Psychologist Skandar said, in the voice adults are required by law to use when they recount what it was like when they were kids, which is a cross between the voice you might use to describe a pony you always wanted and the voice you might use to threaten burglars with injury if they don't leave your house immediately, "I used to watch a TV show called *Mutual of Omaha's Wild Kingdom.*"

"Was that kind of like, um, Six Flags?" asked Henry, trying to seem interested. He figured that was the best way to get this over with. Seem interested and let School Psychologist Skandar have her say.

"No," she said. "*Mutual of Omaha's Wild Kingdom* was not like Six Flags. It was like—life. It was real footage, shot by a real photographer, of real wild animals in real life. It wasn't like this Animal Planet pabulum they feed you kids these days, all cleaned up and family oriented, narrated by a guy with a British accent. No way, Henry, were you gonna turn on *Mutual of Omaha's Wild Kingdom* and see every Tom, Dick, and Mary sticking their hand into a dangerous-looking crevice and pulling out a cute little toad, which somebody planted there thirty seconds before the camera started rolling. Uh-uh, Jack, the *Wild Kingdom* was nature, red in tooth and claw."

"Boy, howdy!" said Henry, trying to get into the spirit of School Psychologist Skandar's story. She smiled at him appreciatively.

"And you know what those animals on *Wild Kingdom* did out in nature, Henry?" asked School Psychologist Skandar.

"No, ma'am," said Henry.

"They ate each other," she said.

"Huh," said Henry. He had not foreseen the story going in this direction.

"Because that's what life is like, Henry. It's dog eat dog. Or lion eat little baby zebra. Or coyote eat little baby lamb, or hyena eat little baby antelope, or shark eat little baby—"

"OK!" said Henry, shifting around on his seat

uncomfortably. "OK, School Psychologist Skandar. I think I get where you're going."

"I mean, I used to watch *Mutual of Omaha's Wild Kingdom* on Saturday evenings with my Oreos and my glass of milk, and I'd see those dingoes circle around that little baby wallaby and close in for the kill, and I'd say, 'Why doesn't the guy with the camera save the little baby wallaby? Why doesn't Marlin Perkins—he was the host; he sat in his Land Rover watching the whole thing while he ate peanut butter sandwiches—why doesn't Marlin Perkins fire up his Land Rover and run over those dingoes and *save* that little baby wallaby? Or why doesn't he at least send his assistant, Jim Fowler, to help?'"

"Well," said Henry, "why *didn't* he run the dingoes over and save the little baby wallaby? Why didn't he send Jim to help?"

"Because," School Psychologist Skandar said, "that's not what nature intended. Nature intends for the weak to *adapt*. Nature doesn't think we're doing the weak any favors by getting them out of jams. Maybe Marlin Perkins could've saved that little baby wallaby with his Land Rover, but when he and Jim and the guy with the TV camera packed up and flew back home to Omaha, what would happen then? Well, the dingoes would still be lurking in the bushes, wouldn't they? Only now they'd be *mad*. Because Marlin Perkins couldn't hang around all the time in the outback providing security for little baby wallabies, could he?"

"I guess not," said Henry. "He had the TV show to put on, and all."

"Darn tootin'," said School Psychologist Skandar. "I think you understand me perfectly."

"Well, I'll look for reruns of the real-life, old-fashioned *Omar's Wild Kingdom* on the Rerun Channel," said Henry.

"*Mutual of Omaha*," said School Psychologist Skandar.

"*Mutual of Omaha*," said Henry.

"Henry," she said, "I think maybe you *don't* understand why I told you this story."

"Not really," confessed Henry.

"Because *you're* Marlin Perkins," she said.

Henry checked himself over. He took a good look at School Psychologist Skandar, who still looked very pretty, even with the gold tooth, and who also looked more or less sane. "No," he said, "I don't think I *am* Marlin Perkins, School Psychologist Skandar."

"You're Marlin Perkins," she said, "and Jurgen is the baby wallaby. And Theotis is the—"

"Dingo," concluded Henry, finally getting School Psychologist Skandar's point. "OK. Yeah. Now I see what you mean."

"I'm glad to hear it, Henry," she said. "Now, various witnesses have assured me that you were only trying to help when you tried to save the little baby wallaby, I mean Jurgen, at the bus stop, but now I have to ask you to quit butting in and let nature take its course, and quit infuriating the dingo. That is, Theotis."

"Yes, ma'am," said Henry. "Is that all?"

"I don't know," rejoined the psychologist. "Is it?"

"Yes," said Henry. "Yes, oh yes, oh yes, ma'am, it is."

A Little Poem

But letting nature take its course turned out to be darned hard to do. At first, complying with School Psychologist Skandar's order seemed like just the ticket. What a great way for Henry to stay out of Theotis's way and improve his chances of achieving plainness!

But in practice, it wasn't that easy. Only ten minutes after he left School Psychologist Skandar's office, Henry encountered Theotis T. Otis the Third along with his girlfriend, Shirley Tantrum, sneaking up behind Jurgen in the lunchroom, carrying a water balloon filled with a liquid Theotis had collected by wringing out the socks of the entire football team into a bucket. Theotis raised the balloon high above Jurgen's unsuspecting little egg-shaped head while Shirley giggled, and then—

"Theotis!" said Henry. He couldn't help himself.

Theotis stopped. He shifted the water balloon to his left hand and made a big, meaty, painful-looking fist with his right. He seemed to be thinking about punching Henry. But he also seemed to be afraid to punch Henry. So he hesitated, at least for a second.

Shirley Tantrum tapped her foot. She was just about out of patience with Theotis, even if he *did* have the most adorable lock of hair in Pumpjack, Texas. Partly, this was because he wouldn't call her "Snookums" anymore. Partly, it was because Theotis was becoming a laughing-stock, thanks to Henry. And partly it was because loyalty was not one of Shirley Tantrum's virtues. So, for all these reasons, Shirley Tantrum disappeared into the crowd, deserting Theotis and leaving him to face Henry on his own. She won't be appearing in this story anymore.

Meanwhile, Theotis began to boil as he thought about how Henry had shown up only a day ago and had already totally made him look dumb at the bus stop, and just now made his girlfriend disappear into the crowd. After Theotis got mad enough to overcome his fear of Henry, he drew back his fist.

"Hold on a second," said Henry, even though he was sure that at any moment his face would begin to hurt. "I need to tell you something."

"What?" said Theotis, his fist wavering.

"Leave Jurgen alone," said Henry.

Meanwhile, a voice in Henry's head was shouting, *This is NOT plain! Don't do it. STOP! Besides, what did the school psychologist just tell you about Omar?*

"Leave Jurgen alone, or what?" asked Theotis. "You're gonna tell everybody the nickname I call my girlfriend? Well, guess what? They already know it. And plus, I don't have a girlfriend anymore." He looked over the crowd a little wistfully in the direction Shirley had taken.

"But still," said Henry, "you have to ease up on Jurgen. And everybody will be much happier. Especially you."

"Are you threatening me?" asked Theotis. It wasn't a rhetorical question. Theotis wanted to know the answer.

"Can you please let Jurgen go?" requested Henry. "Don't make me resort to extreme measures."

The whole school had gathered round.

"So help me, Cicada," said Theotis, "I'm gonna wipe the floor—"

"Really," said Henry. "I don't want to unleash this on you."

"—with your—" continued Theotis.

"There once was a boy named Theotis," began Henry.

Theotis had given him no choice but to break out the ultimate weapon against buffoonery: limericks.

Worry lines broke out on Theotis's habitually blank face. He dropped his meaty fist to his side in confusion.

"Whose friends were revolted to notice," Henry continued.

"Wait," said Theotis, glancing around at the eager people who'd collected up to watch.

"His fancy new pants
Were infested by ants."

"Please," said Theotis. More people gathered. "I'll throw the water balloon in the trash."

But Henry ignored him and kept right on composing poetry. He didn't necessarily want to. He didn't really think it was fun dismantling Theotis piece by piece. But once art starts to happen, there's no stopping it.

"Though the poor boy appeared not to know this."

Theotis froze. He stared at Henry.

From somewhere in the center of the gathered audience, a giggle floated upward, and it spread.

Slowly, Theotis's eyes began to water as the theoretical poetical ants swarmed around inside his new Dallas Cowboys warm-up pants, imaginarily biting more viciously by the second. Theotis twitched. He shivered. He shuddered. He squeaked. "No way," he gurgled in a miserable voice. Grinding his teeth in agony, Theotis plopped the balloon on a nearby table and reached down to scratch.

The whole lunchroom burst into laughter.

The balloon rolled off the table and splattered all over Theotis's shoes. Which Shirley used to really like, back when she was his girlfriend, because they had cost two hundred and fifteen dollars.

Theotis slunk away through the crowd.

Henry glimpsed School Psychologist Skandar standing near the fire exit, shaking her head ruefully. He glanced around for Jurgen, but Jurgen was nowhere to be seen.

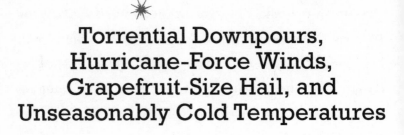

Torrential Downpours, Hurricane-Force Winds, Grapefruit-Size Hail, and Unseasonably Cold Temperatures

Henry rode the bus home, but Jurgen wasn't on it. By the time he walked up the front sidewalk of 339 Bill Street, his mind was going in more directions than a top quark in a supercollider. Lulu, Jurgen, Theotis, Tiffany. General Hedgerow, School Psychologist Skandar, the International Space Station. Elktonium, Raisin, the Giant Tire Emporium, Mayor Fontaine, and . . .

A furious barking came from behind Henry's front door.

. . . Pim Pom!

For one perfect second, Henry forgot everything as he opened the door to find Pim Pom wagging his entire body in greeting. He didn't know if anybody had ever been this happy to see him in his entire life. Henry picked Pim Pom up. Pim Pom kept wagging. All of him. Henry was afraid he might wag himself clean apart, so he squeezed gently to calm Pim down, and felt joy emanating from his puppy's heart like heat waves from a very small star.

"Well," said Henry, "I feel better." He put Pim Pom down. "But I better get started. I've got a lot of things to fix." Pim Pom turned around and trotted down the hall with Henry at his heels.

At the kitchen table, Henry made a to-do list on a Post-it:

Rescue Lulu from Tiffany Glint.

Save Jurgen from Theotis.

Be just plain plain.

Wow. He was surprised to see that he'd put being just plain plain all the way down at number three. Maybe it was fading in significance because of newer developments? Henry really didn't know, because things in his brain were swirling too fast.

Still. Maybe he could do all three things at once? Or did number three contradict number one and number two? Who knew? It was a list, wasn't it? The whole point of a list was, you were supposed to start at the top and cross things off one at a time, not worrying about the stuff at the bottom until you came to it. Right?

With that in mind, Henry contemplated the first item. Rescue Lulu from Tiffany Glint. He couldn't think of any way to accomplish this without actually going to Raisin. The pyramid was one possible way to get there, but he didn't know if he could depend on it, since it had been out of order that morning, and besides, even if it worked, it would only land him inside Lulu's imagination, which was a tough place from which to battle Tiffany. And on top of that, there was no guarantee it was going to take him back to Lulu's imagination again anyway. He had no idea where its flight plans came from, or what they called for.

Maybe, Henry thought, he could ask his dad to drive him. And drop him off at the Giant Tire Emporium.

"Dad?" called Henry down the basement stairs. But his dad didn't answer. Still attending to the community's Slurpee needs at the 7-Eleven. He hung his Phillies cap on the hat tree by the front door. In the hall mirror, he noticed with surprise that all of a sudden his hair was growing back. His cranium looked like a baby coconut.

Well, at least he was making some sort of progress.

In the kitchen, while he impatiently waited for his dad to get home, Henry turned his backpack upside down over the breakfast table. Out fell the book he'd borrowed from the school library during study hall: *The BFG* by Roald Dahl. In addition, on a hunch, Henry had also checked out a few more books about giants: *Jack the Giant Killer*, *Jack and the Beanstalk*, and *Sinbad in the Island of Giants*.

Maybe he'd inherited outrageousness from his mother, but from his dad, Henry had inherited the ability to look up important information from reliable sources. And in study hall, Henry had suddenly realized there was a theme running through the mysterious shenanigans of Tiffany Glint, a theme he should look into further: giants. The Giant Tire Emporium. The Giant Tire Giant. *The BFG* in Tiffany's purse.

Plus, there was all Tiffany's derisive talk of Lulu's *giant* feet and six-foot-plus frame.

As he studied the topic of giants, Henry realized that, overall, these were not good guys. "Fee, fi, fo, fum, I smell the blood . . . ," etc.

Also, apart from being villains most of the time, they seemed to have something else in common, although he couldn't put his finger on what it was. He grabbed the Bible his grandmother had given him when he was seven, and there, in the book of 1 Samuel, was Goliath—not exactly Prince Charming, either. He perused *Harry Potter and the Order of the Phoenix*, which features not only Hagrid but also his half brother Grawp, a giant. And even Grawp, who Hagrid claimed was basically a good guy, well, you had to admit, Grawp was no Mr. Sunshine.

What was going on here? Henry wondered. What was Tiffany Glint's angle, making Lulu into a Tire Giant?

Henry turned to *The BFG*, the book he'd seen protruding from Tiffany's purse. "I is a very mixed up Giant!" proclaimed the BFG, and Henry realized that not even the Big Friendly Giant escaped the general fuzziness of mind suffered by most giants.

Henry went back to the story of Goliath. "Come on, Goliath," he said. "How are you just going to stand there gawking while a kid brains you with a rock? What's going on in your head?"

Slowly, Henry started to understand. Not much was going on in their heads.

It must get to you after a while, he mused. Being a giant. Always feeling different. Constantly wondering what everybody thought. Perpetually asking yourself what the stares were about. Speculating about the whispers. The jeers, taunts, and sidelong looks. Sticking out all the time, literally. *Imagining* just how different you looked in the eyes of others. It could wear you down mentally,

Henry realized. Put cracks in your imagination. And if somebody you had always thought was your friend— somebody you trusted—for instance, your aunt—put the squeeze on your already strained imagination by ridiculing you and tormenting you—calling you a galumphing stork—

"It could do some serious damage," concluded Henry.

"Henry, I'm home!" called his dad.

"Dad, can we go to Raisin, Texas?" asked Henry.

His dad set down a 7-Eleven bag full of Special K breakfast bars as well as the afternoon newspaper on the table next to Henry's books. That's right. Pumpjack, Texas, was a very tiny town, but it was also sort of old school, so it still had two newspapers, one for the morning and one for the afternoon. "Sure!" Phil said. "A road trip! Just like your mom used to like!" A wistful expression crossed his face.

"Although maybe it's not a good idea," backpedaled Henry when he saw Phil's wistful expression. "'Cause you've got work to do in the basement and all. But I just want to—"

"It's a fine idea!" said Phil. "It's totally all right!" He gazed at Henry with the look that reminded him how much he resembled his mother.

Henry realized his newly sprouted hair really hadn't gained him much ground in his mission to stop reminding Phil of Melissa. Sure, now that he wasn't bald anymore, he didn't look like his mom had looked when she was bald. He looked like she'd looked when she had hair.

Phil had begun rooting in the coat closet. "We'll need this canteen," said Phil. "It's made of Elktonium. So remember not to put lemonade in it. And this compass. It doesn't always point north. Possibly because it's made of Elktonium, which seems to have a mind of its own. But still, it points north a lot of the time. And these Elktonium binoculars. Sometimes I see funny things in them. But overall they should come in handy. Maybe we can use them one evening to look for those ghost lights people are always talking about. And maybe this Elktonium whisk? In case we decide to make scrambled eggs?"

"On a road trip?" asked Henry.

"I mean," said Phil, studying Henry's doubtful expression, "no, not if, um—"

Henry glanced at the newspaper on the table. "What? Oh, no!" he cried.

Phil had a look. He read the headline out loud: "'Torrential Downpours, Hurricane-Force Winds, Grapefruit-Size Hail, and Unseasonably Cold Temperatures.' Don't worry,

Henry," he said reassuringly. "My Subaru is a match for all that. Plus," he said, rooting around in the closet, "Elktonium gaiters!"

But Henry wasn't looking at the weather headline. He had noticed a feature in the lower right-hand corner of the front page about a drinking straw that, at approximately 8:59 that morning, had been driven through a two-by-four somewhere out in the wild countryside of West Texas, near a town called Decathlon, by a desert wind. The headline was accompanied by a photo that showed, sure enough, at an establishment with a sign out front proclaiming "SeeFood/Get Gas," a red-and-white straw (not the kind with the flexible elbow) that'd lodged itself in a board. But Henry hardly glanced at the much-ballyhooed drinking straw, because in the background of the picture, parked beside a gas pump, was a Plutonium Pink HumZee Exploder with a kayak strapped to the top. The unmistakable profile of Tiffany Glint slouched behind the steering wheel. And struggling to remain upright in the high wind while fueling up the HumZee was Lulu. "They were on the outskirts of Decathlon," murmured Henry. "Wherever that is. Buying more gas. They're not in Raisin anymore."

Henry's dad was testing an Elktonium umbrella.

"Should we get started packing for our road trip to Raisin?" asked Phil.

"You know what, Dad," said Henry softly. "Never mind."

"But we— What if— I have all these things," said Phil, hopefully presenting Henry his Elktonium armload.

"It's just that—" said Henry, unsure how he was supposed to explain why, since he'd asked if they could go to Raisin, he no longer wanted to go to Raisin. "I changed my mind?" He could only stand and watch silently as Phil sadly replaced all his Elktonium implements in the closet. "Well, I think there are a few toaster strudels mixed in with the Special K bars I brought from the 7-Eleven," Phil said when he was done stowing the Elktonium. "Why don't we have dinner?"

When the strudels popped out of the Elktonium toaster, Henry's was dark, his dad's was light, and Pim Pom's was medium, exactly the way they each preferred. Ignoring the overpowering scent of Mr. Clean that came from the hot toaster, Henry smeared the three pastries with margarine from a light brown tub.

As they ate in silence, a knock came on the back door. Before anyone could answer, Jurgen Mintfarm scurried in.

"Toaster strudel for dinner?" asked Jurgen.

Henry and his dad nodded.

Pim Pom just kept on chowing down.

"Awesome," said Jurgen.

"Would you like a toaster strudel?" offered Phil.

"Sure," said Jurgen. "I like mine—"

"Don't worry," said Phil. "It'll come out just right." He dropped in a strudel, pushed down the Elktonium lever, and the strudel disappeared into the machine. "So," said Phil while they waited. "You two know each other?"

Henry and Jurgen both nodded.

"Are you—friends?" Phil asked.

His face aimed at his plate, Henry secretly looked at Jurgen through his eyebrows. Jurgen looked back. Neither of them answered.

"I mean, do you—like each other?" asked Henry's dad, making things more awkward by the second. "Do you hang? Are you tight? Henry, is Jurgen your dog?"

"No, Mr. Cicada," said Jurgen, pointing at Pim Pom. "I think that's Henry's dog."

Henry's dad said, "OK, boys." His expression grew distant. "Looks like you've got things under control. I'm going down to the basement. Got an idea for an Elktonium nose clamp. You know, the kind you use when you swim." He went down the stairs.

"Dad!" yelled Henry. "You already invented that!" To Jurgen, Henry said, "Do you even *use* a nose clamp when you swim?"

"Are you kidding?" Jurgen answered. "Aren't there enough reasons for people to make fun of me? Besides, I think people quit wearing nose clamps to swim sometime in the 1970s."

"That sounds about right," said Henry. He hadn't been around in the 1970s, but he'd seen pictures. Long lines of cars at the gas station, knee-high athletic socks, people sporting nose clamps at the pool. "My dad spends a lot of time in the basement," Henry added.

"Mine's usually hiding in the garage," said Jurgen.

They sat in silence for quite a while, during which time Jurgen showed no sign of leaving.

"Listen," Henry finally said. "I'm sorry. I'm sorry I didn't act friendly at the bus stop, or on the bus, or at school, or after school."

"You really didn't," agreed Jurgen. "But unfriendliness is not the reason I came over."

"Then why?" asked Henry.

"I came because I'm worried," said Jurgen.

"About what?" asked Henry.

"Your hearing," said Jurgen. "School Psychologist Skandar only has one speech. And I've heard it. A bunch. It's about *Orval's Wild Kingdom*. So I know exactly what she said to you in her office, and I'm afraid you didn't understand."

"Omar," said Henry. "It's *Omar's Wild Kingdom*."

"Didn't she tell you about the dingo?" demanded Jurgen. "Didn't she tell you about the little baby wallaby? Didn't she tell you to let nature run its course? Didn't she tell you to lay off Theotis?"

"Yes," said Henry. "She told me all that. But it's hard to do. I was only trying to help."

"You didn't help," said Jurgen. "You have never helped. So stop *trying* to help. Because of your 'help,' Theotis is sitting in a folding chair on my sidewalk right now, smacking his knee with a kettledrum mallet. I can't go home."

"Have you got a back gate you could use, maybe?" asked Henry. "Or a hedge to climb through? Or—have you got an underground tunnel?" The sun had dropped quite a bit in the evening sky. Hmm. Henry noticed it was nearing the spot where it'd been when the pyramid opened its eye the night before. So—wow—this would *really* be a good time to go have a look and see what Pim Pom's doghouse was up to. Before the sun descended much farther. Because maybe it was a long shot, but he hoped it might take him to Lulu again, wherever she happened to be. Henry shot Jurgen a friendly but meaningful look. Its meaning was: *Good-bye! I've got stuff to do!*

But Jurgen had no intention of leaving Henry's safe kitchen and going home, where Theotis was probably waiting with a baggie full of substances he'd collected off the floor at the Greyhound station. "Listen," he said. "Maybe I'm small, and maybe it's easy for oversize boneheads like Theotis to push me around, but that doesn't mean I'm just going to grin and bear it. I think the Founding Fathers were smack on the money when they said I have a right to life, liberty, and the pursuit of happiness. So the way I see it is, you got me into this, and it's only fair for you to get me out."

"I don't think the Founding Fathers had this kind of situation in mind when they wrote that," observed Henry.

"I think they did," retorted Jurgen.

"It's just that—I'm on a quest," explained Henry.

"What kind of quest?" asked Jurgen.

Henry was tempted to tell Jurgen the truth about Lulu. He seemed just weird enough to understand. But Henry couldn't be sure, so he just said, "To be plain *plain*."

"How's it going?" asked Jurgen.

"Not too well," admitted Henry.

"I would have to agree," said Jurgen.

Henry drummed his fingers on the table and calculated how much time he had before the sun dropped to the horizon.

"You did this to me," Jurgen said, "with your brilliant but irresponsible limerick."

"Sorry, Jurgen!" cried Henry. "I have to go somewhere!" He bolted for the backyard, where, in the rays of the setting sun, dangling a little over six degrees above the edge of the horizon, the pyramid had begun shimmering like mad.

At the same moment, in the basement, yet another stray shaft of evening sunlight filtered through the window and lit upon a shard of Elktonium glittering on Phil's workbench. Phil saw it. The spectacle once again inspired him to slide the Elktonium sample under Melissa's old quarktronic microscope. It glimmered and pixelated and turned from iridescent green to pearlescent pink. And as it did, Phil saw the clever little atoms of Elktonium rearranging themselves into the shape of something familiar, and that was when he made his second discovery about the hidden properties of Elktonium.

"Slingshots," he marveled. "Tiny slingshots. You could even say—nanoslingshots."

Phil's thoughts went back to a time when he was a little boy, and he had a slingshot of his own. He remembered a particular incident in which he'd accidentally let go of the handle, not the sling. The whole contraption flung itself backward into his skull and ricocheted high into a tree. Because *a slingshot can sling itself.* And that's exactly what these tiny Elktonium nanoslingshots seemed poised to do. Sling themselves.

Phil wondered what would happen if somebody arranged those slingshots into the perfect formation, with the angles just right, so they slung at exactly the right tilt at exactly the right time. What if there were a way to aim them all at once toward the forty-seventh, forty-eighth, and forty-ninth dimensions? Maybe if they were organized into a cube? Or an octahedron? Or a dodecahedron? Or a tetrahedron, which is commonly called a "pyramid"? There was no way for Phil to tell, really. The answer to his question wasn't visible through the microscope. Still, Phil couldn't help wondering: When conditions were ideal, energy levels just right, forces aligned perfectly, would they be able to sling themselves (and therefore the structure they'd been arranged into) somewhere really cool?

And if somebody happened to be sitting inside the cube, dodecahedron, or tetrahedron (that is to say, pyramid), well, then, would the nanoslingshots sling the somebody, too?

Phil considered hollering at Henry to come look. Then he shook his head and told himself, "That's nuts. No way anything like that could ever happen. Besides. Henry's tired of hearing about Elktonium." He switched off the microscope and got busy whittling an Elktonium toenail clipper, knowing all the while in the back of his mind that his project was doomed to failure.

"Hey!" Jurgen panted, chasing Henry out of the kitchen. "Stop trying to ditch me!"

In the backyard, Henry sprinted toward Pim Pom's doghouse. Jurgen, who was faster on his feet than he looked, followed close behind, and as Henry dove for the door, Jurgen, refusing to let Henry off the hook, dove after him.

Pim Pom barked warily, but he followed, too. Henry was the best friend he had.

No Damsel

This," said Jurgen, wedged tightly inside the doghouse, as he extracted one of Henry's elbows from his ear, "is weird."

Pim Pom wiggled between them looking for room to breathe.

"It's about to get weirder," said Henry, watching the last of the day's sun rays creep across his backyard.

"How?" asked Jurgen, squeezing into a pyramid corner so Pim Pom could move his hind leg to scratch a flea.

"It just will," said Henry. "Buckle your seat belt. The ride is gonna be a little bumpy."

Pim Pom whined softly as if in agreement.

"Wait," said Jurgen. "Your dog is crazy, too?"

"Crazy," said Henry, "is what's about to happen, buddy."

The sun continued to drop in the west. Nothing happened, except the skin of the pyramid crawled with pearlescent pixels.

"Any time now," said Henry. Nothing continued to happen.

"Fun stuff," observed Jurgen.

"Wait. I thought I had it all figured out," said Henry. "I thought the pyramid would work when just the right shade of sunlight hit it at exactly the right angle."

Pim Pom began absentmindedly trying to dig a hole in the floor. He seemed pleased with his results, although they were more or less invisible to the naked eye.

"Sure. Right. Listen," said Jurgen. "Maybe I'll just wait outside in the yard. It's crowded in here."

"Good idea," said Henry. At that point, even more nothing happened.

"Pardon me," said Jurgen, trying to squeeze past Henry.

Which was when something happened.

The sun dropped half a degree and its light hit the pyramid at an infinitesimally changed angle. *Take us to Lulu*, Henry thought. *Take us to Lulu*. And then they were swept away on a strawberry-tangerine aura, their toes (even Pim Pom's, all twelve) curled with the acceleration.

Jurgen screamed, "OK, OK, OK, I believe you, I believe you, I believe you. It *is* crazy!"

Pim Pom howled in fright.

And Henry thought of Lulu. Was she all right?

Then came the free fall. Henry whispered to Jurgen, "Get ready. We don't know what conditions might be like when we arrive. Lulu's mind could've collapsed almost totally by now. She's been alone with her aunt for a while. No telling what kind of torment the evil Tiffany Glint has inflicted. Lulu is really tall, and Tiffany calls her a 'galumphing stork.' So take a deep breath, Jurgen. Get ready, Pim Pom. I feel us coming in for a landing. It could be a rough one."

"Whose mind? Collapsed how? The evil Tiffany Glint? What does any of that mean?" asked Jurgen.

"Just keep your wits about you," said Henry. "And follow my lead."

There was a gentle bump. The doghouse grew dark and silent.

"What now?" asked Jurgen. "Is the teleportation over? Are we on an alien planet?"

"Shhh," said Henry. "Let me scope things out. Hold on to my belt. Yank me back in if I shout for help."

"Sure thing," said Jurgen, grabbing on.

Henry eased out of the doghouse. What he saw shocked him.

Behind him, Pim Pom crawled from the door cautiously, and Jurgen followed.

"Oh, man," said Jurgen. "You were right! How could things be any worse?" They stood in the calm, quiet ballet studio. Stravinsky poured from the ghostly piano. "Ewwww! Ballet? Yuck! Classical music? Gawwww!" said Jurgen.

"This—isn't exactly what I was talking about," said Henry. "This isn't what I expected. I mean—it was a ballet studio when I left last time. I just didn't expect it to be in such good shape."

"I hate ballet—" began Jurgen.

"Oooh," howled Pim Pom.

"Shhhhhh," said Henry.

"Henry!" said Lulu from the dimness. "Is that you?"

"Whu-whu-whu-what was that?" stammered Jurgen, glancing around for the source of the disembodied voice.

"You mean *who* was that?" asked Lulu indignantly. "I'm a person."

"Hi, Lulu," said Henry.

"Hi, Henry," said Lulu.

"Jurgen," said Henry, "meet my friend Lulu. Lulu,

meet my friend Jurgen," said Henry.

"Graaaak," said Jurgen. "Where are we?"

"We're in Lulu's imagination," explained Henry.

"Wh-wh-who is Lulu?" Jurgen managed to spit out.

"Like I said, a friend of mine," replied Henry.

"I didn't know you had any friends," said Jurgen. "Besides your dog."

Pim Pom rubbed against Henry's leg.

The light from the windows dimmed and then brightened again.

"What was *that*?" cried Jurgen.

"Those are the windows that are Lulu's eyes," said Henry.

"I'm just gonna sit in this wooden chair for a minute," said Jurgen faintly.

"That's fine, because Lulu and I kind of have a lot to talk about, so if you listen to our conversation, you'll probably get the big picture, and I'll fill in all the missing details when we're done," replied Henry. Through the corner of one of the windows that were Lulu's eyes, Henry glimpsed Tiffany at the wheel of the HumZee. He thought he saw her shoot a sidelong glance his way.

"Are you OK, Lulu?" asked Henry.

"Yes, I am," replied Lulu brightly. "Why wouldn't I be?"

"Because—you're in the clutches of your aunt Tiffany, and your parents are headed for space, and the last time I was here, your imagination was squashed down to the size of a thimble, and you were a Tire Giant, and—"

"That was then," interrupted Lulu briskly. "And this is now. Aunt Tiffany apologized. She saw the error of her ways. I helped show them to her, actually. So things are back to the way they used to be when I was little. Everything worked out fine."

"Well," said Henry, "that's good news. I guess."

"You guess?" echoed Lulu.

"I mean—yeah. I'm glad things are fine," replied Henry. "I just think—that was kind of a sudden turnaround on Tiffany Glint's part, wasn't it?"

"Maybe," said Lulu. "But I'm happy. I don't like to fight with Aunt Tiffany."

"Hold on," said Jurgen. "Let me get this straight. Her aunt is the evil Tiffany Glint? The one you told me about?"

"Unfortunately," said Henry out of the side of his mouth, "yes."

Lulu heard them. "Stop!" she cried. "You guys don't call Aunt Tiffany evil! I told you! She apologized! She's had a hard life! She hasn't had the opportunities! She hasn't had the advantages! She's doing her best! She's try-ing! For your information, she's taking me to the Young Ballerinas of America Competition!"

"Really?" asked Henry.

"Really!" Lulu shot back.

"Lulu—I mean—don't take this the wrong way—but is this a good idea? You haven't had many lessons," said Henry. "Or any lessons. Other than watching PBS and YouTube videos. Right?"

A crack appeared in the ceiling of Lulu's imagination.

"Do you know what your aunt's really up to?" Henry pressed.

"Henry—" whispered Jurgen, pointing to the crack. "Did you make that happen? With all your questions? Cause maybe you'd better stop asking."

"Yes, I *do* know what Aunt Tiffany is up to, Henry!" cried Lulu. "She recognized my potential. She made a video. She sent it off to the judges, along with a note vouching for my skill. And *they* recognized my potential, too. They told Tiffany so. They let me into the competi-tion. And now Tiffany is taking me there. She did this all for me in secret, and then surprised me with the news!"

Henry could see Tiffany watching Lulu out of the cor-ner of her eye again. She smiled. Whatever she was seeing on Lulu's face, she liked.

"Does her story really make sense?" asked Henry.

"Or," continued Jurgen, "is the evil Tiffany Glint just telling you what she thinks you want to hear so she can manipulate you even more awfully?"

Henry, Lulu, and Pim Pom briefly fell silent to contemplate Jurgen's insightful point.

"People have been mean to me in a lot of different ways so far in my life," explained Jurgen. "So I'm kind of an expert."

"I think Jurgen is right, Lulu," said Henry. "I think you're getting into deep trouble. I think Tiffany may still be trying to collapse your imagination. And somehow, a place called Nowhere could be mixed up in all this. I don't have every single detail. But whatever she's up to, it's no good."

"What are you talking about? Nowhere? Where do you get this stuff?" asked Lulu.

"From a guy in my shrubberies," murmured Henry.

"Oh, that's great, Henry," said Lulu. "Sounds like a reliable source. This is really rich, coming from you. You think I need you to ride in here like a knight in a shining doghouse with your friend and your little pet and rescue me?"

"Maybe," said Henry.

"I'm no damsel in distress, buster," boomed Lulu inside her head. "Maybe *you* need somebody to rescue *you*! Did you ever think of that?"

"Actually," said Henry, "yes."

But Lulu didn't hear him because she was still busy yelling at him inside her head. "Look at yourself!" said Lulu. "What do you see? I'll tell you what you see!"

"Henry, how does she know what you look like?" asked Jurgen.

"You ever hear of a mind's eye, Jurgen?" Lulu asked.

"Yes," replied Jurgen.

"Well, I'm looking at Henry through my mind's eye," Lulu snapped. "Moping around inside my head with that porcupine hair. And I'm looking at you, too, Jurgen. And wondering what's up. Because Henry says you're his friend, even though you don't think he *has* any friends. I just heard you say it."

"I said no friends except for *Pim Pom*," corrected Jurgen.

Lulu plowed on. "Before you come in here telling me I need to be rescued from my aunt, who actually cares about my dance career, because she sent in a video and got me into an important contest, maybe you ought to look at yourself in the mirror!"

Henry checked his reflection in the wall of the dance studio. "I'm the first to admit," said Henry, "I'm not looking that good."

"Nope," snapped Lulu. "You're not."

"Who you talking to, Lulu?" Henry heard Tiffany ask from outside. "People inside your head?"

"Nobody," said Lulu. "I'm talking to nobody."

"Yes you are," said Tiffany. "You got an imaginary friend?"

"Henry Cicada," murmured Lulu. "Only he's not imagina—"

"Blah-hah-hah-hah!" interrupted Tiffany. "Cicada! That's the name of a big old bug!"

"He said it was *his* name," replied Lulu.

"Suit yourself, Longlegs," drawled Tiffany. "I mean, Lulu. I mean, honey. Whatever points your toes!"

"Maybe you better just go, Henry," Lulu said briskly inside her head. "Nice meeting you, Jurgen. Bye-bye, Pim Pom."

The doghouse began to glow on the studio floor. The eyeball seemed to be studying new travel orders written in the distance. After a pause, it gave Henry a meaningful stare.

"Whoa," said Jurgen, taking in the eye. "Didn't notice *that* before. Looks like it's trying to tell us something."

"It's trying to tell you to leave," said Lulu.

"Wait!" cried Henry. "Lulu! I'm not imaginary! I mean, I'm not just a figment! You're not, either!"

"I know I'm not just a figment, thank you," said Lulu tiredly.

"He's definitely not just a figment," threw in Jurgen.

"Whether you're a figment or not a figment doesn't really matter right now," said Lulu. "I need you to leave so I can concentrate on my performance."

"We inhabit the same dimensions!" persisted Henry. The eyeball glared. Henry herded Pim Pom and Jurgen into the pyramid and climbed in after them. "I saw you in my dad's afternoon paper! Tiffany is up to something, Lulu!" he called out the door.

But the doghouse had already begun whooshing them through the cosmos.

Highway 99999

"**O**K," said Jurgen as they tumbled over one another into Henry's yard. "That went well. Whatever it was, it went really, really well."

"Shut up," said Henry.

Pim Pom searched for a tree, but settled for a bush.

"Henry, you're *almost* a good guy," observed Jurgen. "You're close. But you're not *actually* a good guy, because you never really make friends with anybody, do you?"

Pim Pom, back from his visit to the bush, whimpered, because he was Henry's friend.

"Anybody *human*, I mean," added Jurgen, patting Pim Pom's head. "It always seems like you've got something more important on your mind."

After a moment, Henry sighed. "You're right, Jurgen."

He climbed his kitchen steps. Jurgen followed. Inside, Henry dredged a handful of maps out of a drawer and located one for West Texas. "But all that's about to change."

"What are you doing?" asked Jurgen.

"I'm going to find Lulu," replied Henry, unfolding the map on the breakfast table.

"If she didn't want you in her imagination, is she going to be happy when you show up in her life?" wondered Jurgen, eyeing the map.

"Probably not," allowed Henry. "But it's a chance I gotta take. I think she's headed for real trouble."

"Like what?" asked Jurgen.

"I don't know what," replied Henry. "But maybe I know where."

"No!" exclaimed Jurgen. "Where?"

"Right," said Henry.

"Huh?" asked Jurgen.

"Nowhere," said Henry.

"You just said that," said Jurgen.

"I know," said Henry.

"Know what?" asked Jurgen.

"Nowhere!" said Henry.

"Well," said Jurgen, "this has sure been fun, but can

we switch to another word?"

"I know it sounds crazy," said Henry. "But the name of one particular place keeps coming up. General Hedgerow said it. School Psychologist Skandar knew about it. It's a place where people end up when their imaginations are in trouble, I think. Nowhere."

"Is it as bad as it sounds?" asked Jurgen. "With a capital letter and everything?"

"I think it may be worse," said Henry.

"You know," mused Jurgen, "I would have to agree with that, even though I don't totally understand what I'm agreeing to. Kind of like when I signed up for youth hockey in Amarillo. Had to checkmark those boxes holding all parties blameless and stuff. And then some guy broke my ankle with a stick. Anyway," he added as Henry rifled through the map drawer some more, "I'm coming."

"You're staying," said Henry. "You don't want to go where I'm going."

Jurgen thought about it. "No. Not really. I mean, not if it's like that last location you teleported me to."

"It's not a teleporter," said Henry. "What are you, some kind of nut who watches the Syfy channel all day long?"

"Yes," said Jurgen.

"It's a doghouse," said Henry. Frantically, he searched

Google Maps, Goggle Maps, Apple Maps, and Orange Maps on his iPhone. No Nowhere. "It's a pyramidal Elktonium doghouse," he clarified.

"A doghouse that takes you inside the imagination of a girl," said Jurgen, "who is really, really tall. And possibly headed Nowhere."

"Well," said Henry, "yes."

"And you say *I'm* the nut," observed Jurgen wryly. "She seemed kinda nice, Henry, even though she was mad at you. Is she really in trouble?"

"I'm afraid I turned the dingo into a mad dog," lamented Henry.

"You were listening to Skandar after all?" asked Jurgen.

Henry nodded.

"Aunt Tiffany is the dingo-slash-mad dog?" said Jurgen.

"Yep," said Henry. "And Lulu is the wallaby. Now let's get to work. No location known as 'Nowhere' seems to appear on any modern map of West Texas. But look," he said, spreading out the old gas station map. "Here's Decathlon. Where the newspaper photo placed Lulu and Aunt Tiffany Glint sometime around eight fifty-nine this morning." He glanced at the clock. "It's now seven fifty-three p.m."

"There's only one road leading through Decathlon, Texas," noted Jurgen.

"Highway 99999, running east to west," said Henry. "They must've been traveling down it. All we've got to do is get on 99999 and go!"

Jurgen looked at Highway 99999. "There's five hundred miles of Highway 99999," he said. "In Texas alone. If they went west, it took them through Dustbowl and Sandpile and Skylab and El Paso and ten other towns. And if they were going east, it took them to Dryden, San Antonio, Houston, or Galveston."

"True," said Henry.

"And even if we knew whether they went east or west," said Jurgen, "how do we know they didn't turn north or south at the first crossroad they came to?" He consulted the map. "And go to Stockpile, Barracuda, Nopalo, or Saltine?"

"I don't know how we know," said Henry. "I guess we don't know." He sighed.

"And even if we knew whether they started off going east or west, and even if we knew whether they turned north or south at the first crossroad, how do we know they didn't turn east or west again at the next *criss*-crossroad?"

"I don't know that, either," said Henry.

"Basically, Lulu could be anywhere in Texas," observed Jurgen.

"I guess so," said Henry.

"And, wait, look, Henry. Then there are all these roads in the mountains that don't exactly go north or south or east *or* west, but kind of squiggle around in every direction and come out in Mexico," said Jurgen.

"Jurgen," said Henry, "could you please shut up?"

"I'm just telling it like it is," said Jurgen.

"Let's have some jerky and go over it all one more time," said Henry. "Maybe there's something we missed. Can you remember the name of that ballet competition Lulu mentioned?"

"Nope," said Jurgen.

"Raaaargh!" said Pim Pom, scenting the jerky.

Much later, the sound of footsteps came from below, and Henry's father emerged from the basement door carrying an Elktonium dog dish. He blinked at the boys in surprise. "What time is it?" he asked.

"Oh, it's just ten fifty-one," said Henry casually, as if 10:51 weren't really very late for a school night.

"OK," said his dad, starting out of the kitchen. "Ten fifty-one. That's not very late for a—" Then he stopped.

"Wait. Ten fifty-one? Ten fifty-one *is* very late for a school night, Henry. Shouldn't you be in bed?" He started out of the kitchen again. Then he caught sight of the map. "You boys studying Alaska in school?" he asked, stopping to have a look.

"This is a map of Texas, Dad," said Henry.

"Ah," said Henry's father. "So it is," he said. Turning away, lost in his own Elktonium-centered thoughts, Henry's dad absentmindedly filled the Elktonium dog dish with water and set it under the table for Pim Pom, who lapped it up enthusiastically. "Well, I'm off to bed. Good night, Pim Pom. See you in the morning, Henry. Nice to meet you, Bjorn."

"Jurgen," said Jurgen.

"Jurgen," said Henry's dad. "Good night."

And Henry's father went to bed happy, a little bit, as happy as he felt like he was allowed to be, all things considered, because his son had a friend, a regular friend, the kind you stay up late studying geography with.

Henry and Jurgen silently pored over maps of Texas a while longer. After Henry felt sure his dad was asleep, he rounded up half a jar of peanut butter, an Elktonium knife, and the Elktonium binoculars. He found a nearly full bottle of orange juice in the refrigerator and dumped the haul in his backpack. He also tore out the newspaper photo of the drinking straw stuck into the two-by-four in Decathlon, with Lulu, Tiffany Glint, and the Plutonium Pink HumZee Exploder in the background, and brought it along.

"You're really doing it?" asked Jurgen.

Pim Pom ran to the back door and pressed his nose against the wood. He was ready for action.

"I'm really going to find Lulu," said Henry.

"But we still haven't figured out," said Jurgen, "how you know you'll find her if you go."

"I don't know I'll find her if I go," said Henry. "But I know I *won't* find her if I don't go."

"That's logical," said Jurgen.

"Sure is," said Henry.

"Only," said Jurgen, "maybe there are some things you haven't thought of."

"I'm sure there are," said Henry, "but I'm still going."

"I'm coming with you," said Jurgen.

"Better not," said Henry.

"I can't go home. Theotis probably booby-trapped my sidewalk. Besides, don't you want company?" asked Jurgen.

Actually, Henry did. Because he was more than a little

scared. "OK," said Henry. "But you have to promise to be careful and do everything I say."

"I promise," said Jurgen.

"Let's go," said Henry. "Pim Pom, you're staying here."

Pim Pom whined indignantly, as if to say, "Listen, guys, it's no fair leaving me here, since it *was* my doghouse that started all this, even if my doghouse is made of something that I still find slightly unsettling."

"OK then," said Henry to Pim Pom, scribbling a basically truthful note to his dad saying not to worry if he didn't seem to be in his bed the following morning, because he was really just going Nowhere to check on his friend Lulu and planned to be back soon.

"You can come, too," he told Pim Pom, who wagged himself and grinned.

"What are we gonna do?" asked Jurgen as they slipped out the back door. "Hitchhike?"

"No," said Henry. "I think I know where we can borrow a set of wheels."

How Many Man-Traps
Were There?

Henry didn't see any sort of knocker or doorbell on General Hedgerow's slightly haunted-looking house. He *did* see a little brass ring, which, when he pulled it, turned out to be attached to a thin iron chain that led through the wall and was itself attached to something inside that sounded like a sink disposal grinding up rusty SPAM cans.

"That's his doorbell?" asked Jurgen as what appeared to be a bat fluttered out of the shrubs and rowed upward toward a broken window in General Hedgerow's second floor, where it plopped onto the sill and crawled inside like a leather crab.

When there was no response, Henry muttered, "OK, where were those man-traps?" He eyed the tarpaulin-cloaked form of the Muckeridge-Pressley. "And how many man-traps were there?"

"What *is* a man-trap?" asked Jurgen as he wandered around General Hedgerow's driveway.

Henry, lost in thought, began perfecting a plan to avoid the man-traps. The plan involved a trained garden snake, three fifty-pound bags of flour, and a mashie niblick. He failed to notice Jurgen wandering across General Hedgerow's driveway and grabbing the tarpaulin that covered the Muckeridge-Pressley. Henry did notice, though, when Jurgen suddenly flew ten feet into the air and dangled upside down in the night sky by his ankles. "Yow!" shouted Jurgen. As the tarpaulin trailed from Jurgen's fists, the Muckeridge-Pressley shone under the streetlights in all its glory, bright orange, polished to a high gloss, and boasting nearly one whole horsepower.

Looking closely, Henry could see that Jurgen's feet had been caught in a noose of nearly transparent nylon rope he must have somehow triggered by fiddling with the Muckeridge-Pressley. Well, that took care of one man-trap.

"Get me down," hissed Jurgen.

Right about this time, Pim Pom saw the scooter and the sidecar attached to it. Ancient dog-circuits fired in his brain. Wind in the face, tongue flapping in the breeze, all that great canine stuff. He streaked across the driveway and leaped for the sidecar, but at the precise instant his three padded little paws left the ground, an iron cage sprang from the pavement like the jaws of an enormous crocodile, snatching him out of the air and imprisoning him like an unruly orangutan at the zoo. So there was the second man-trap.

Maybe, thought Henry, *the coast is now clear*. He inched carefully toward the bike. Cautiously, he searched the Muckeridge-Pressley for the starter button. Pim Pom whined softly. Jurgen struggled with the nylon rope. "Sorry, boys," Henry whispered. "But you'll have to wait till I get the Muckeridge-Pressley started. I hope you've sprung all the man-traps." As Henry circled around the motorbike checking it for hidden buttons, knobs, or levers, he found a mushy spot in the driveway, and, realizing it was the trigger to the final man-trap, stepped carefully around it. At that second, the front door of the house flew open and out blustered General Hedgerow in his pink-and-white-striped pajamas. He'd fallen asleep in front of *Base-Camp Gourmet*, and hadn't heard Henry ring his so-called doorbell.

"Oh," he bellowed, "I say. This is brilliant. Eleven thirty-one in the night and out to pinch my motor?"

"General Hedgerow!" shouted Henry.

"Stick a cork in it, boy," said General Hedgerow. "You've gone too far!"

"No," said Henry. "*You've* gone too far. . . ." But it was too late. General Hedgerow, not paying attention to where he was walking, stepped on the trigger of his final man-trap, and *whang*! A little yard gnome standing innocently by the mailbox flung a meat cleaver, a hatchet, a carving knife, and the blade of a World War II bayonet at General Hedgerow, pinning him to the wall by his shirtsleeves and pant legs.

"Yaaargh!" exclaimed the general.

"Sorry, General Hedgerow," said Henry, "but I just wanted to borrow the Muckeridge-Pressley. You said I could ride it. Let me help you down from there."

"Borrow the old M-P?" said General Hedgerow. "Whatever for?"

Wiggling the bayonet out of the woodwork to free General Hedgerow's left pant leg, Henry launched into the short version of the story. "You see," he said, "there's this girl, and she's kind of nice, and kind of in trouble, and we think the evil—or at least really really bad—no, definitely evil—Tiffany Glint has kidnapped her, even though she won't admit it—"

"Stop!" bellowed General Hedgerow. Henry stopped working on the bayonet. "You're off to aid a woman?"

"Yes," said Henry. "I guess that's about the size of it."

"You want to watch the damsel-in-distress folderol," advised the general. "Don't get carried away. People don't always appreciate it."

"I've run into that," said Henry.

"I'm guessing with the young lady in question?" asked the general.

Henry nodded as he resumed working the bayonet out of General Hedgerow's pant leg.

"Yes, well, the whole concept is considered rather old-fashioned, I'm afraid," said the general. "Damsels these days don't often want or need to be saved, or even referred to as 'damsels.' Though it's still a worthwhile quest in my opinion, if approached with decorum, respect, and a spirit of cooperation. Do hurry with that."

"She doesn't need me to *save* her," said Henry. "She just needs my help."

"Capital!" roared the general. "Well said."

Henry wiggled the knife back and forth faster. It was really stuck in the garage door.

"Frankly, my boy," observed the general, "you seem rather impaired."

"I do?" asked Henry.

"What with the grief, the dejection, the sadness, the regrettable attempts at conversation undertaken between you and your father—" continued the general.

"How do you know so much about me?" asked Henry. "Are you some kind of spy?"

"Couldn't help hearing through the hedge, couldn't help seeing through it, you know," said the general. "And actually, I *am* some kind of spy. Retired. Only trying to help, though. What I mean to say is, according to my observations, currently you may not be at your best."

"He's not," confirmed Jurgen.

"Right-o," said the general. "However, in my experience, sometimes a harebrained rescue mission is just the thing to snap us out of our darker interludes."

Henry pulled the knife loose. "On second thought, better put it back, Henry," said the general.

"Why?" said Henry.

"Because," said the general, "if I were free to move about, and a young neighbor of mine and his two friends came to steal my M-P for an ill-advised attempt to help a female in distress, which he probably hadn't told his father about—"

"I left a note," interjected Henry.

"Aherm, I'm afraid I'd be honor-bound to oppose him, no matter where my sympathies actually lay," declared General Hedgerow.

"I see," said Henry, sticking the bayonet back. "Thank you for understanding, General."

The general just rumbled like a distant atmospheric disturbance.

Quickly, as General Hedgerow, Jurgen, and Pim Pom watched, Henry undid the clamps holding the zeppelin-shaped sidecar on to the Muckeridge-Pressley. He removed it and carefully leaned it against the wall of General Hedgerow's house. He scampered off to his own back-yard and returned lugging Pim Pom's doghouse. Sticking it into the three clamps that used to affix General Hedge-row's sidecar, Henry battened the pyramid firmly to the bike.

"Yes, and about that sort of thing," began the general. "Your pyramid. Aherm. I have noticed certain peculiarities through the hedge that cause me concern."

"You mean the eyeball on top?" asked Jurgen.

"Among others," said the general. "The forces you find yourself dealing with call for restraint. Caution, sharp wits, a clear head. I did some work along those lines for the Queen of England."

"What kind of work?" asked Jurgen.

"Missing persons," said the general.

"Who was missing?" asked Jurgen.

"Winston Churchill," said the general. "After World War II. The genuine Winston Churchill disappeared, you see. I mean, a shell of him remained with us. But major aspects of the man had vanished."

"Like what?" asked Henry.

"Like his imagination," replied the general, "ergo, his greatness."

"Did you find him? Or his missing aspects?" asked Jurgen.

"We suspect we had located the general vicinity of their disappearance," said the general, staring off to the west. "And in the process, we found a dimension, or two, or forty-six, that people had previously been unacquainted with, not to mention approximately one hundred ghostly blue lights."

"Well, that's really interesting," said Henry distractedly, "but right now, I have to go find Lulu."

"Tallyho and all that," said the general. "We must each find our own way. No use overwhelming you with unnecessary guidance."

Henry stopped and looked at the general. "I appreciate

that, sir," he replied.

"Starter button's on the handle grip, right side, Henry," continued General Hedgerow.

Henry started the bike.

"Eaglesburger Triple-Amplified Crystal Set mounted there on the handlebars. It's an old-fashioned radio. Over the years, a few of the crystals have burned out, but it still may be worth a listen. Possesses special capabilities."

Henry took note of the egg-shaped device glowing on the handlebars.

"If you clap your hands three times loudly, it'll deactivate those two man-traps in the driveway," said the general. Henry clapped three times. Jurgen fell ten feet onto the yard, which, it turned out, was pretty soft, for a desert, but what was really impressive was that he managed to do half a flip and land on his feet. Pim Pom leaped up and down joyfully when the cage released him and returned to its pothole. General Hedgerow, though, remained pinned to the garage door by sharp objects.

Henry fiddled with the different levers, knobs, and switches on the handlebars of the Muckeridge-Pressley. He didn't exactly know how to ride a motor scooter, much less a 1942 Muckeridge-Pressley with a pyramidal doghouse attached.

"Front brake on the right," said General Hedgerow. "Clutch on the left."

"Clutch?" Henry said. "What's a clutch?"

"The clutch," General Hedgerow explained patiently, "is the lever you happen to be squeezing with your left hand. When you release it, the Muckeridge-Pressley will begin moving forward."

Henry let go of the clutch. Sure enough, the Muckeridge-Pressley lurched down the driveway toward the street.

At just about the same moment, a large cement truck with the logo "Theotis T. Otis II Concrete Company" spinning slowly around on its drum turned the corner. The truck made its way up the street on a collision course with Henry and the Muckeridge-Pressley.

"Figures," muttered Henry, seeing the name on the side of the truck that was about to mash him to jelly while making a cement delivery at night.

"Watch out, Henry!" shouted Jurgen.

"The clutch, boy, the clutch!" shouted General Hedgerow. "Use the clutch. And the brakes! Don't forget the brakes!"

"Arf, arf, arf!" barked Pim Pom.

Henry yanked on what he thought was the clutch

lever and stomped on what he thought was the brake. But he was getting panicked, and he couldn't quite remember what was what, and he did everything backward, pretty much, which only made him speed faster toward the oncoming truck. He tried dragging his large canvas shoes on the driveway, which slowed him down maybe a little, but not enough. He was headed straight for the radiator grille of the cement mixer.

Fortunately, at the last second, Henry's brain started to work again, and he turned sharply to the right. The Muckeridge-Pressley tipped dangerously up on two wheels. The Elktonium pyramid rose high in the air. Almost immediately, the old M-P plowed through the general's prized geranium plant and then flattened his mailbox, shuddering to a halt and coming down with a bounce on all three tires.

"Bravo, Henry!" said General Hedgerow as the cement mixer rumbled safely past. "I like that. Quick thinking in the face of danger."

"Thanks, General Hedgerow," said Henry shakily.

"But perhaps, on second thought," said the general, "you'd rather unpin me from the woodwork and let me drive you on your quest?"

"No, sir," said Henry. "I gotta do this myself."

"Right you are!" bellowed General Hedgerow. "What was I thinking? Jolly good! Squeeze the clutch lever to change gears. Shift with your left foot. Kick the lever up for first gear, and stamp downward upon it for two and three. Twist the throttle once you've got her in gear."

"Twist the what?" asked Henry.

"The throttle is the right handle grip," advised the general.

"Cool," said Henry.

Jurgen and Pim Pom climbed carefully into the doghouse, which Henry had installed with the door facing backward.

"Another thing," said General Hedgerow. "There's a small box of Royal Marine Rocket Flares under the seat. Might want to take them with you. Fire them out the back of the doghouse in a pinch. Give you a nice little boost. Only make sure you've got, say, thirty to fifty miles of good, straight road ahead of you before you light one of the little blighters. More, if at all possible."

"Thanks, General," said Henry.

"One final bit of advice, Henry," called the general. "When traveling where you're about to travel. Know what you're doing. Be sure. No waffling, noodling, or shilly-shallying. You don't want to get caught halfway between.

Neither here nor there. Because that's Nowhere."

"Uh-huh," murmured Henry, his thoughts already somewhere over the horizon.

"But wait! Nowhere is exactly where Henry said we're—" began Jurgen.

Whatever else the general had to say was lost in the buzzing of the old M-P's .9 horsepower engine. They were off.

Midnight Special

Highway 99999 led out of Pumpjack between two small mountains made of ghostly white stone. Beyond the stone mountains, there was nothing but darkness.

In that darkness, Lulu awaited.

As Henry hummed across the blacktop, peering deep into the night as far as the Muckeridge-Pressley's four-candle-power headlamp would reach, watching for squirrels, deer, and javelinas in the roadway, he didn't know what would happen. He didn't know if he'd find Lulu before Tiffany did something atrocious to her. He didn't know if he'd *ever* find Lulu.

Maybe she didn't need to be found. Maybe her aunt really wanted the best for her, and her ballet career, and her life.

But Henry didn't think so, and there *was* one thing he knew for sure: he was doing something. And that was a lot more fun than doing nothing.

So they motored through the night, guided by the wavering yellow beam of the old M-P headlamp. Later, when the sun began to rise and it was easier to see, Henry, Jurgen, and Pim Pom had decided, they'd ignite one of their rocket flares and try to drive a little faster.

And after a long while, when Henry could begin to make out, by the glow of the rising sun, a length of straight black highway stretching all the way to the horizon, he rapped on the side of the doghouse. Inside, Jurgen and Pim Pom got busy. Jurgen wedged the nose of a Royal Marine Rocket Flare in the front corner of the pyramid, pointing the tail out the back, and Pim Pom sat on it to keep it from flopping around when it fired. Jurgen searched his front pants pockets for matches. But Jurgen had no matches in his front pants pockets. Or in his back pockets. Or in any other pockets.

"Henry!" Jurgen shouted out the door of the doghouse. "Got any matches?" Henry checked both his pockets. At the same time. He probably should've kept at least one hand on the handlebars. Then he might not've driven the scooter off the road, into the ditch, and through a roadside miniature golf course based on the theme "Gopher Holes." Boy, was that a rough ride. The rattling, bouncing, jouncing, and shaking threw Pim Pom and Jurgen around the inside of the doghouse like so much underwear in a tumble dryer. Henry bounced thirteen feet out of the Muckeridge-Pressley saddle.

In the midst of all this, Pim Pom's third left toenail on the rear skittered along the Elktonium floor of the doghouse, sending out a plume of sparks worthy of a Perseid meteor. One of the sparks landed on the fuse of the flare, ignited it, and just as Henry was coming down from thirteen feet high to land on his can, the flare shot the scooter right underneath him.

In less than a second, Henry found himself traveling at a rocket-assisted sixty-six and two-thirds miles per hour (the speedometer had spun one entire time around, and then another), and just as he managed to steer the old M-P back up on the road, he hit ninety-nine and three-thirds (the speedometer made another revolution), which is the same as a hundred miles an hour. And the rocket was just *starting* to burn.

In the doghouse, it sounded like somebody flying a jump jet around inside a wishing well.

Henry had just watched his speedometer make its

fifth lap around the dial (one hundred sixty-six and two-thirds miles per hour) when he looked up to see an elderly woman pushing a baby carriage across the highway four miles ahead. Unfortunately, the scooter immediately hit one hundred ninety-nine and three-thirds (or two hundred) miles per hour, and kept accelerating. Henry drove it off the road to avoid hitting the lady and her baby carriage. All in all, that was probably for the best, although if Henry had known the carriage was only filled with old bread-wrapper ties, he might not have worried so much about making sure not to run over it.

Closing in on three hundred miles per hour, which is about how fast many airplanes fly, Henry, Jurgen, and Pim Pom crossed the fields of nineteen goat farmers, who had fortunately left all their gates open, so the old M-P passed easily in and out. About the time the speedometer hit three hundred thirty-three and a third miles per hour, Henry somehow found himself right back in the proper lane of Highway 99999, headed west. He breathed a sigh of relief, and let go of the handlebars to knock twice on the wall of the doghouse, which was the signal to Jurgen and Pim Pom that everything was all right. Unfortunately, when Henry let go, he very nearly blew right off the back of the old M-P. So after that, he just held on with both hands and enjoyed the ride.

Those three boys mogatered on down the road.

What does "mogater" mean? Well, let's listen as two older Texans use it in conversation. Mr. and Mrs. Orrin Festival happened to be standing in the darkness beside Highway 99999 when the M-P screamed past, examining their mailbox, which had been blasted full of shotgun holes by passing motorists. Why are Texans so hard on rural mailboxes? You'll have to ask one of them. I don't know.

"Look at them boys mogater!" said Mr. Festival admiringly to his wife, Doreen, as the M-P faded into the distance.

"Ninety-to-nothing!" replied Doreen.

"Reminds me of when I was a kid!" said Mr. Festival, and slapped his knee.

"If you was my kid, I'd tan your behind," replied Mrs. Festival.

Leaving Mr. and Mrs. Festival to finish their conversation, and rejoining Henry, we see him approaching a highway sign: "Danger, 33 Miles."

Almost immediately, Henry saw another sign: "Danger, 23 Miles." And then, a few eyeblinks later: "Danger, 13 Miles." Then: "Danger Ahead."

Henry was pretty sure "Danger" wasn't just the name of another Texas town, although you never could be sure in these parts.

Then Henry saw a stop sign approaching really, really fast. Beyond it, a monstrous pile of rocks that'd slid off the face of a roadside cliff blocked both lanes of the highway. Henry braced himself and wished there were some way to tell Jurgen and Pim Pom to do the same.

And then, just in the nick of time, the rocket flare sputtered out. Pretty soon they were going thirty-three and a third miles per hour again, then less, and less, and less. Henry rolled to a stop at the stop sign.

"You guys OK in there?" he asked Jurgen as he pushed the Muckeridge-Pressley around the rock slide on the shoulder of the highway.

"That was *so* darn scary," said Jurgen, sticking his head out of the pyramid to chat.

"Not to mention incredibly dangerous," added Henry. "You guys didn't even *see* the rockslide coming, did you?"

"Awooo!" wailed Pim Pom, poking his head out.

"I was *sure* we were goners," said Henry, as he steered past the last few boulderous bits of the rockslide and rolled the old M-P back up onto the highway.

"Rrrrr," said Pim Pom, shuddering.

"Wow," said Jurgen, mopping the sweat off his brow. "Oh, man."

"Oh, man," said Henry, shaking his head to clear away the cobwebs of fear. "Wow."

"Aieeee!" moaned Pim Pom, covering his eyes with his paw.

"Ready to do it again?" asked Henry.

"Absolutely," said Jurgen, breaking out another flare.

"This is not at all plain," observed Henry. "So can we keep it to ourselves once we get home?"

"Sure thing," agreed Jurgen.

"Arf, arf!" barked Pim Pom excitedly, his toenail poised to strike the spark.

"Let her rip!" said Henry.

When that particular flare sputtered out, they found themselves forty miles farther out in the wild, dry, strange, and wonderful heart of West Texas, at a crossroads. Henry looked at his watch. It wasn't even six a.m. yet.

He squinted around at the dim desert and put the Elktonium binoculars to his eyes.

"Are those Speculoculars?" asked Jurgen.

"They're actually just binoculars my dad made out of

Elktonium," said Henry, "and all I can see through them is prickly pear."

"No," said Jurgen, examining them, "those are Speculoculars. As in speculative binoculars. They see alternative future worlds. They show you what *might* happen, if something were to go a little differently than planned in this world. They show you *what if.* They show you a world of speculation. . . ."

Henry had taken the Elktonium binoculars, or, if you please, Speculoculars, down from his eyes and was staring at Jurgen. "Where do you come up with this stuff?" he asked.

"Some dude on the Syfy channel had a pair last week. He was using them to explore the six thousand most probable iterations of the jungle planet Bilge," said Jurgen.

"Oh, great," murmured Henry. "The Syfy channel again."

"Believe me or don't believe me," said Jurgen. "I don't care." Suddenly, a worried look crossed his face. "Is today Thursday?"

"Yep," said Henry.

"I just thought of something I need to do," said Jurgen. He climbed inside the doghouse as a blazing ball of morning sun cleared the mountains to the east, casting down a slanting beam on them from an angle of six degrees, and the sky above them became the strawberry-tangerine of daybreak. "Hey!" Henry said. "Hold on!"

Henry saw the skin of the pyramid begin crawling with shimmering pearlescent pink pixels. The eye appeared at the top, gazing toward the north, and almost immediately, Henry saw the glow of strawberry-tangerine light through the doorway of the doghouse. "Jurgen!" he shouted. "Out of the doghouse! Where's Pim Pom? Is he in there, too?" But it was too late. The whole house, with Jurgen and Pim Pom inside, disappeared.

Because the sunlight *does* turn strawberry-tangerine for a few seconds at sunrise, just like it does at sunset. Henry didn't spend much time thinking this fact over until later.

Meanwhile, Jurgen, the doghouse, and Pim Pom materialized inside the imagination of Mathilda Hatfield, the Pumpjack public librarian, which looked exactly like the actual circulation room of the Pumpjack Public Library, except there were no left-behind umbrellas in the umbrella stand.

Peering out her eyes, which seemed to show him everything Mathilda could see through her half-moon reading spectacles, Jurgen whispered, "What happens if Jurgen Mintfarm doesn't get a chance to turn in *Have Space Suit—Will Travel* by Robert Heinlein before tomorrow?"

He watched through the spectacles as Mathilda's fingers pulled up his library membership on the circulation computer. His heart sank as she placed her pinkie on the Delete button.

"NO NO NO!" cried Jurgen as loudly as he could in Mathilda's imagination. "Jurgen will get it back in time!"

Mathilda's finger hovered. She hesitated. Finally, she harrumphed and closed the screen without deleting Jurgen's account.

"Phew," said Jurgen, and the doghouse winked at him and took him back to the desert.

He climbed out, Pim Pom on his heels.

"Am I ever glad you guys are back," said Henry. "Where'd you go?"

"To the imagination of Mathilda Hatfield," said Jurgen.

"Hmmm," said Henry, thinking. "The doghouse didn't take you to Lulu? It took you to Mathilda Hatfield? Who is Mathilda Hatfield?"

"The librarian of Pumpjack," said Jurgen. "I have an

overdue book I'm worried about."

"How overdue?" asked Henry.

"Tomorrow makes two years," said Jurgen.

"You need to get it together, man," advised Henry.

"So what I did was," continued Jurgen, "when the doghouse took me inside the imagination of the librarian, I asked what would happen if my book weren't returned by tomorrow, and then when I looked out her eyes, I saw her canceling my card. I think I managed to talk her out of it for now, from inside her head, but do you think we can get back by tomorrow?"

"Maybe," said Henry. "But in the meantime, we should try to figure out what your library trip *means*. About how the pyramid works, and how all this adds up."

"That could take a while," said Jurgen. "It seems pretty complicated. But going on information I've picked up from the Syfy channel, I believe that the pyramid is somehow able to sense our destinies and help us reach them. Maybe. Possibly. Or maybe not. The wisdom of the Syfy channel is deep, complex, and often difficult to decipher."

"We'll have to think all this over while we drive," said Henry, eyeing Jurgen contemplatively. "But right now, we have to keep moving or we'll never find Lulu. Mount up."

They did. Jurgen broke out another rocket flare, noticing that their supply was dwindling. He stuck the nose of the rocket into the front corner of the Elktonium doghouse and Pim Pom sat on it. Henry clamped his fingers around the Muckeridge-Pressley handgrips, and Pim Pom struck a spark with his toenail. Almost immediately, they were going approximately 667 miles per hour.

Meanwhile, less than forty miles away, Lulu sat silently beside her aunt Tiffany as Tiffany piloted the HumZee Exploder through the desert landscape, singing her little heart out. The air conditioner blew through Tiffany's straw-like hair and the morning sun blazed in the blue sky. The song Tiffany sang was—well, it's kind of hard to say what the song was, because Tiffany was a terrible singer. However, it sounded happy.

After a while, Tiffany stopped singing. "We'll be at your big contest, soon, Lulu," she said. "I'm pretty sure we're headed in the right direction now. You ready for your big day?"

"Are you sure it's OK that I haven't taken any real lessons and just learned dance steps from watching videos?" asked Lulu. Somehow, this had all seemed like a better idea hundreds of miles ago when her aunt first talked her into it.

"Absolutely!" replied Tiffany. "In fact, that's probably better!"

But Lulu felt strangely nervous. One, because she'd never danced in a contest before. Two, because in the back of her mind, she wondered if maybe Henry had been right. Maybe there was more to her aunt's sweet behavior than met the eye. It *was* very unexpected, and sort of unsettling. She wished there were some way to get in touch with Henry.

Tiffany glanced at a mile marker. Mile marker 767. "Getting close," she said. "I guess it's time we heard a little more about Mary Stiltskin, Lulu. Can you fill me in?"

"Maria Tallchief?" asked Lulu.

"Yep," said Tiffany.

"Maria was the first American to perform in the Bolshoi Theater of Moscow," began Lulu enthusiastically. "She founded the Chicago City Ballet in 1981. Maria has been honored by the people of Oklahoma with multiple statues and her own day."

"Oklahomans," muttered Tiffany. "Typical."

"What?" asked Lulu.

"Nothing," said Tiffany. "Go ahead."

"Maria was inducted in the National Women's Hall of Fame, and later, she received a National Medal of Arts.

In 1996, Maria received a Kennedy Center Honor for lifetime achievements," concluded Lulu breathlessly. "She was spectacular."

Tiffany Glint looked at her niece with tears in her eyes. "Well," she said. "That is beautiful, Lulu. Thanks for going over the whole dang thing one more time."

Lulu saw her aunt's tears. Then, feeling her own eyes start to water with happiness at the thought of her aunt Tiffany's total change of heart, Lulu looked quickly back at the highway ahead.

"Lovely," said Tiffany Glint brightly. "Great. Maria. Maria Tallchief."

"Thank you for being so interested, Aunt Tiffany," said Lulu. "Thank you so much!" Lulu felt incredibly touched at her aunt's sudden enthusiasm for her favorite subject.

"Man alive," cackled Tiffany Glint, "is Maria ever Tall. Right, Chief? Maria is Tall, Chief. Just like you! Hee hee hee! Tall, Chief. Get it?"

"I guess I get it," replied Lulu hesitantly.

"You wanna be like Maria Tallchief!" declared Tiffany.

"Yes," replied Lulu.

"Well, you *are* like Maria Tallchief," said Tiffany.

"Thank you," said Lulu.

"The tall part, I mean," said Tiffany.

"And," began Lulu, "I'm going to be a—"

"This whole thing is so, so . . . dad-gummed PER-FECT!" burst out Tiffany Glint.

"It really is," said Lulu softly.

"Dang right it is!" added Tiffany, checking a hand-drawn map she'd been looking at repeatedly since they left Decathlon.

"Is everything OK, Aunt Tiffany?" asked Lulu.

But before Tiffany could answer, a terrible sound came from one of the immense tires of the HumZee.

Tiffany pulled over at the very bottom of a burnt-orange hill to check out the noise. "Dang! Flat tire!" called Tiffany. "Lulu, Giant Tire Giants such as you are good at changing flats, aren't you? I mean, *former* Giant Tire Giants?" And she giggled uncontrollably for reasons known only to herself.

Are You an Expert?

Just about the time Tiffany Glint was making Lulu change her tire, Henry, Jurgen, and Pim Pom's next-to-last rocket flare sputtered out, and the old Muckeridge-Pressley rattled to a stop near the base of a dusty orange hill. The sun was now high in the sky, and the desert had begun to warm.

Jurgen and Pim Pom stepped out of the doghouse to stretch their legs. Henry picked up the Speculoculars. "No," he murmured as he scanned their surroundings. "Nothing. Nothing, nothing, nothing."

"What are you speculating when you look through them?" asked Jurgen.

"I'm just wondering, 'Where is Lulu?'" replied Henry.

"That's not a speculation, that's a question," observed Jurgen. "Come on. Let's drive to the top of this hill. We'll be able to scan more territory. So we'll have a better chance of seeing something when we *speculate*."

Henry started the little gasoline motor of the Muckeridge-Pressley, which was the only way to make it go if you didn't want to burn a rocket flare. The M-P sputtered to life, and Henry let out the clutch. The scooter putted for thirty-nine feet and then it died. Henry tried to start it again, but no dice.

Jurgen unscrewed the fuel cap. "Henry," said Jurgen. "We're out of gas. Maybe we should use the last rocket flare to get to a service station."

"No," said Henry, staring up the road. "Not yet. Let's just get to the top of the hill and have a look around with the Speculoculars, like you said. We're close to Lulu. I can feel it." So Henry pushed the right handlebar, Jurgen pushed the left, Pim Pom stuck his nose against the back fender, and the three of them rolled the old M-P upward.

From the hilltop, Henry scanned the desert again. "Nothing," he muttered. "Still nothing, nothing, nothing."

"Give me those," said Jurgen, reaching for the Speculoculars.

"What for?" asked Henry.

"I don't think you're using them right," Jurgen told him.

"Why are you an expert on Speculoculars?" Henry asked peevishly. "Because you watch the Syfy channel more than all the members of the science club, the chess team, and the Junior Space Explorers put together?"

"I've been thinking this over," replied Jurgen, ignoring the insult because he was pretty sure Henry didn't mean it, plus, it was darn close to the truth, "and I think if *I* were using the Speculoculars, I'd look through them and ask a *speculative* question like, 'What would it look like *if* I found Lulu?'"

"So?" snapped Henry.

"So while I was watching the joyful reunion the Speculoculars had shown me in answer to my question," replied Jurgen, "I'd also kind of look around behind the reunion or to the left or right of it to see if I could spy a highway sign or a street sign or a city limits sign or some other kind of landmark. Then I'd know *where* the joyful reunion was taking place, Henry, and if I knew that, I'd know where to go to find Lulu."

Henry snorted derisively. "Well, Mr. Genius, I thought you said Speculoculars show you 'what if,'" he said. "They can't just show you any old thing you wish you knew."

"Weren't you listening?" asked Jurgen, getting mad,

too, because his journey so far hadn't exactly been a trip to Disney World. "I just said 'what if.' *What* would it look like *if* I found Lulu?"

"But the *what* and the *if* aren't next to each other!" retorted Henry.

"Oh, now you're criticizing my syntax?" shot back Jurgen.

"Give me those!" hollered Henry, snatching at the Speculoculars and watching in horror as they flew through the air and landed on the highway with a nauseating crunch. He ran to pick them up.

"I'm sorry," said Jurgen. "I'm sorry, Henry!"

"I'm sorry, too, Jurgen," said Henry, as he desperately peered through the cracked Speculoculars, pointing them toward the bottom of the hill. A puzzled frown crossed his face. He lowered the Speculoculars from his eyes, shook them, and looked through them again.

Then he wordlessly handed the Speculoculars to Jurgen, who gazed down the highway in the direction Henry was pointing. Jurgen's mouth dropped open and he handed the Speculoculars back.

Because what they saw through the cracked Speculoculars was Lulu. Right at the bottom of the hill. Changing the tire of a pink HumZee. Tiffany Glint sat on the hood of the HumZee, wearing a scary grin.

"What's going on?" he asked Jurgen.

"Did we break the Speculoculars?" asked Jurgen, shaking them some more.

"Why are they showing both of us this speculative scene?" said Henry. "'Cause the only question I have in mind is: Where is Lulu?"

"That's exactly what I have in my mind!" said Jurgen. "We've got to figure out what this means!"

"Yip! Yip!" said Pim Pom excitedly, pointing his nose downhill.

Meanwhile, at the bottom of the hill, the real Lulu really worked on changing the actual flat tire of the true HumZee, because what Henry and Jurgen were seeing was not speculation at all. Getting dropped might've knocked the speculative function right out of the Speculoculars, the way falling off a jungle gym knocks the wind out of a second-grader, but they were still ocular. Meaning, they were still good for seeing things.

So what Jurgen and Henry were seeing was Lulu struggling to change a tire, which was hard for her because Tiffany Glint had already misplaced the tire tool that the HumZee factory had included when they manufactured her buffoon car, and all Lulu had to work with was a rusty Stillson wrench that'd fallen from the pocket of her Giant Tire Giant coveralls, which Tiffany had wadded up and stowed in the kayak, for some reason.

The Last Flare

"**H**old on a second," muttered Henry, glancing down the hill with unaided eyes. "Maybe I'm going crazy, but I still see her!"

"And maybe I'm going crazy," added Jurgen, "but so do I."

Pim Pom just pointed his nose at Lulu and barked exuberantly as she climbed into the HumZee.

"Pim Pom sees her, too," noted Henry, "and we can't all *three* be nuts."

"We'd better get down there quick," said Jurgen. "They're pulling away."

Without really thinking the idea through, Henry said, "I'll aim the M-P at them. You light a flare."

"It's the last one," said Jurgen. "But here goes!" And

without thinking the idea through, either, he cued Pim Pom to strike a spark with his toenail.

"Arrgfff!" said Pim Pom.

Shoo, Fly

Meanwhile, back in Henry's neighborhood, as clouds gathered overhead, a fly landed on General Hedgerow's nose. But General Hedgerow, still pinned to his garage like a homecoming corsage, couldn't scratch it.

Almost a Year

In the front yard of 339 Bill Street, a gentle rain began, the way rain begins sometimes even in the desert, and Phil Cicada, carrying the morning newspaper inside, turned his face upward to greet it. He realized he felt a little less sad than he had the day before.

"Wow," said Phil to himself. "That hasn't happened for almost a year."

Then he went inside.

Audacious, Outrageous,
Courageous

By the time Henry, Jurgen, and Pim Pom got to the spot where the HumZee was parked, they were going three hundred thirty-three and a third miles per hour. There was no way to stop the Muckeridge-Pressley. Not for another thirty to fifty miles. What none of them had thought of was this: you can't just turn a rocket flare off.

So Pim and Jurgen could only stare mournfully out the rear of the pyramid as the Plutonium Pink HumZee faded into the distance.

"Lulu!" cried Henry over his shoulder.

But the M-P kept screaming down Highway 99999.

After many, many miles, but only a few minutes, the rocket began to sputter out. Slowly, and then more and more quickly, the Muckeridge-Pressley lost momentum.

The telephone poles stopped looking like a picket fence, and the dotted line down the middle of the highway began to look dotted again. Eventually, the motorbike rolled to a stop. Unfortunately, there was no more gas in its tank, and there were no more flares in the doghouse, so this was where Jurgen, Henry, and Pim Pom would have to stay.

"We got kind of carried away, didn't we?" said Henry sheepishly. He sat down hard in the dirt. That was when one of the many rain clouds scudding over the desert that day burst overhead and drenched Pim Pom, Jurgen, and Henry with a bone-chilling rain.

The Speculoculars, because they were busted, broken, and possibly still mad at Jurgen and Henry for acting like such numbskulls earlier, refused to show them any more than they could already see by squinting really hard.

"Hey, Jurgen," said Henry, gazing at Pim Pom's Elktonium doghouse with a contemplative expression. Pim Pom scratched at his left leg. Henry picked him up. Pim shivered in his arms.

"What?" asked Jurgen.

"I think I figured something out," said Henry.

"Do I have to figure it out, too?" asked Jurgen, shivering because his clothes were soaked. "Or can you just tell me?"

"The thing is, I'm not exactly *sure* what I figured out," said Henry.

"Well then, can you really claim to have figured it out?" wondered Jurgen.

"It's about the doghouse," Henry went on. "When it took you to the librarian's imagination, did you *need* to go?"

"Y-yes, I did," said Jurgen. "Because I don't know if you've noticed, but I'm kind of a nerd. If I don't have books in my life, I don't have anything."

"No way we're going to let you lose your borrowing privileges," Henry reassured him. "The world needs more nerds like you."

"Th-th-thanks, Henry," said Jurgen through chattering teeth. "I guess."

"Are you cold?" Henry asked. "You're out of fuel. You need food. Eat this peanut butter."

"Do we have a spoon?" asked Jurgen. "Or some crackers to put it on?"

"Got this Elktonium knife," said Henry. "You can dig the peanut butter out and lick it off the blade. Don't worry about cutting your tongue. The knife is as dull as preseason football."

"Thankth," said Jurgen, digging in. "You're not

originally from Texath, are you?"

"Nope," replied Henry. "Wanna wash that peanut butter down with some of this orange juice?"

Jurgen took a swig. "Geh!" he said. "Peanut butter. Orange juice. Aftertaste!"

"OK, forget about the juice," said Henry. "So. Back to Mathilda. Did you really *need* to go visit her?"

"Yeth," said Jurgen, digging in again. "That about thumth up how much I needed to go to vithit her, Henry, at the time the thtrange doghouth took me away and depothited me behind the imadginary thirculation dethk. Like I thaid, I have a book thath two yearth overdue."

"Yeah, that's atrocious," observed Henry.

"I know," said Jurgen.

"All right now," said Henry. "Let's see. I think that doghouse can somehow sense what people need, and give it to them."

"What do you mean?' asked Jurgen, handing Henry the peanut butter. Henry downed a dollop.

"I mean, I think the doghouth, or the Elktonium, or thomething in the Elktonium, can thomehow gueth who we are and what we're like and it can figure out what we need, and it can thend uth to get it," said Henry. "Like it underthtandth the pattern thingth are thuppothed to happen in, the thcheme, the thcheme of thingth."

"Well, that pretty much describes my experience," said Jurgen.

In the sky above, the clouds parted, allowing a strawberry-tangerine beam of sunlight to filter through. It struck the desert floor miles away and began moving steadily toward them.

"PB ith gone," said Henry. "I wish I'd remembered to pack some jerky. It's going to be a long day." He studied the clearing sky. "I wish the pyramid would take me to Lulu," he said. "If I could get to her, maybe I could figure out where she is. But it only seems to work at sunrise and at sunset—"

"—when the light turns strawberry-tangerine," finished Jurgen.

"Right," sighed Henry dejectedly.

"Exactly the same color as that beam of light refracted by the storm clouds," said Jurgen.

"What beam of light?" asked Henry.

"The one headed our way across the desert. That looks like it's going to hit the pyramid in about fifteen seconds," said Jurgen, pointing.

"It *is* the right color!" cried Henry. "But it's not falling at the right angle. The pyramid only seems to activate when the sun's on the horizon. And the rays are hitting it at about, I don't know, maybe six degrees!"

"Get in the pyramid and leave the rest to me!" cried Jurgen.

Henry climbed in. Outside, he heard Jurgen grunt, and he felt the pyramid tilt half an inch.

"Ohhh," groaned Jurgen. "This is heavy—Pim Pom—good boy! Stick your nose right here and push!"

Slowly, Henry felt the pyramid floor slope as Jurgen and Pim Pom heaved it on edge. Just as the whole thing was about to tip over, he saw the strawberry-tangerine ray light up the day outside. Inside, the pyramid began to pixelate its green-y green. Jurgen must've managed to angle it in the sunshine just right.

"Woof," said Pim Pom.

"Good luck, Henry!" he heard Jurgen call.

"Good thinking, Jurgen!" Henry called back, but he didn't know if Jurgen heard him over the swoosh.

When Henry got to Lulu, her imagination was hollow, quiet, empty. The ballet studio had changed. It was much smaller. Instead of occupying an opera house, it seemed to be located in an aging strip mall on a stretch of highway outside a sad, depopulated town, next to a Sonic Burger. A boom box, forgotten in one dusty corner, not only didn't play Tchaikovsky, it wasn't even plugged in. This ballet company had clearly fallen on hard times.

When Henry called Lulu's name, his voice echoed back to him, but she didn't answer. "Lulu!" called Henry again. "Lulu!"

Nothing.

"Lulu," whispered Henry dejectedly.

"Henry!" answered Lulu softly after a short pause. "I'm so glad you came back!"

"Me, too," Henry said. Then he asked, "Where are you? Jurgen, Pim Pom, and I are trying to find you. In the real world. We're worried. Really worried."

"I'm worried, too," said Lulu. "Aunt Tiffany is up to something. She's acting weird. Weirder than she ever has. And she's also acting nice. Nicer than she ever has. Which is even weirder. I'm afraid maybe you and Jurgen were right. Maybe this is all just part of some plan meaner than anything she's tried yet."

"Even if it is, you can stand up to her," Henry reassured her, glancing around at the dusty, decrepit studio her imagination had become after all her worrying. As he watched, a crack appeared in one of the full-length mirrors.

"I wish my imagination were stronger!" cried Lulu. "I wish I weren't a giant."

"Listen, Lulu," said Henry, "you're not a giant. You're just really tall. And it actually seems like your imagination is pretty good. I mean, I know it's always about to collapse because of the escapades of Tiffany Glint, but the thing is, every time I come, it's collapsing in a new and creative way. For instance, now your ballet studio seems to be going bankrupt. I think you just have to be a little more audacious."

"Outrageous?" said Lulu. "Courageous?"

"Exactly," Henry said.

"All right then," said Lulu, "I'll try. I promise. When the time comes, I'll try. But Henry, now I think we should talk about you."

"Why?" said Henry.

"Because I've got a couple of questions for *you* about outrageousness and audaciousness," she said, "and also maybe about courageousness."

"Like what?" asked Henry.

"Like—remember when you told me you make your dad sad?" Lulu asked.

"I remember. I still do—I *still* make my dad sad," said Henry.

"How could somebody like you possibly make any-body sad?" asked Lulu.

"Because I remind him of my mother," said Henry. "I'm like she was. Audacious. Outrageous. Sometimes, maybe, even courageous. Also, there are my glittering eyes, which I can't do anything about. But outrageous and audacious I can keep a lid on."

"If it made your dad happy for your mom to act outrageous, courageous, audacious, and have glittering eyes, shouldn't it make him happy for *you* to be like that, too?" Lulu wondered.

Henry considered this. He thought about it long and hard. He sat there and he was so quiet for so long that Lulu began to worry that she'd upset him. "For the past year, no," he finally said.

"But now," Lulu continued, "isn't it time you started acting like yourself again? Don't you think your father would like to have his son back? Doesn't that make sense?"

"Maybe," said Henry, after a pause, "but what if you're wrong?"

"I really don't think I'm wrong," replied Lulu. "I think maybe your dad isn't the only problem in your house. I think maybe *you're* afraid of outrageousness, audacity, and courage. I think *you* want to take the plain way, because it's the easy way. I think you don't feel like you're allowed to be the same person you were before your mom died. And I think *you* need help just as much as I do. I mean—one day maybe I'm going to be special because I dance. You—you're going to be special just because you're Henry."

"You may be right," allowed Henry.

"I'm pretty sure I am," replied Lulu.

"General Hedgerow warned me about this," Henry said.

"Who?" asked Lulu.

"A friend of mine," replied Henry. "He said that sometimes when you set out to rescue people, it can get a little unclear exactly who needs saving."

"I think we've done each other a lot of good," said Lulu.

"Me too," agreed Henry.

"Orpheum, here we come!" sang out the voice of Tiffany Glint from the driver's seat in a tone reminiscent of a metal shredder.

"What's 'Orpheum'?" asked Henry.

"The name of the theater where my competition is happening," said Lulu.

"So maybe," mused Henry, "if Jurgen and I can figure

out how to get to the Orpheum, we'll see you there. Where's the Orpheum?"

"I don't know," said Lulu. "I don't even know if Aunt Tiffany is sure. She seems a little lost."

The pyramid pixelated as the eyeball scanned something invisible in the distance. New flight instructions, Henry figured, because almost immediately, the eyeball looked at him and raised its eyebrow meaningfully. "Hold on," Henry told it. "I have to figure out where Lulu's headed."

The eyeball glared and the pyramid pixelated furiously, as if saying, "Don't argue with me, kid." Henry knew the last thing anybody needed was for him to miss his cosmic ride, so he called, "I'll find you, Lulu," and climbed inside. In less than a second, he was hurtling away through the dimensions.

A Sign

Meanwhile, beside Highway 99999, Jurgen and Pim Pom had seen a sign. Actually, they had seen two signs, one on the left side of the road, one on the right. They didn't see angels in the sky or a burning bush on a mountain or a ram in a thicket or any of the other stuff people are prone to see in the desert. No, Jurgen and Pim Pom saw a neon sign blink to life atop a hill in the distance. It read "SeeFood/Get Gas." On the facing hillside glowed one that said, "BE   ART."

"Hold on—" Jurgen said.

The doghouse materialized. Henry tumbled out. "Lulu's in trouble," he barked. "We have to get to her."

"When?" asked Jurgen.

"Now," said Henry.

"Any idea where to look?" asked Jurgen.

"The Orpheum Theater," said Henry.

"Never heard of it," said Jurgen.

"We've got to think," said Henry. "Hey. Haven't we seen that vista before?" He pointed to the faraway signs.

"I was just thinking the same thing when you materialized," said Jurgen.

"Woof," said Pim Pom.

"In my dad's newspaper," Henry remembered.

"Yeah," said Jurgen. "That picture we were looking at right before you went nuts and dragged us all on this bizarre field trip. The one of the drinking straw in the two-by-four. That showed the HumZee with Lulu gassing it up. It was taken right there, at SeeFood/Get Gas."

"By the way, this is not a field trip," said Henry. "Also, I warned you not to come."

"I'm not saying I didn't want to come," said Jurgen. "Because I did. I'm just saying it's bizarre, that's all."

"Besides the emergency tire change, that restaurant/gas station is one of the last known stops Lulu and Tiffany Glint ever made. Let's go check it out," Henry proposed, digging the newspaper clipping from his backpack to compare to the scene in front of them. "Maybe the guy at the cash register heard them say something important."

"And maybe we can have dinner while we're there?"

hinted Jurgen, who was starving.

"I don't think there's time for food," Henry said. "But we better Get Gas."

"Arf," said Pim Pom. Henry reached down, and Pim Pom leaped into his arms, wiggling with joy and licking Henry's face with his warm rose-petal tongue. Henry felt better about things.

The gas station/restaurant seemed to be only a couple of hilltops away, but in the desert, distances are hard to judge, and hills can be far apart. It took them half an hour of pushing the old M-P to reach "SeeFood/Get Gas."

"Please Wait to Be Seated," read a sign by the counter.

A huge aquarium full of giant goldfish greeted customers. While Henry and Jurgen waited, they watched the fish. A coconut tree rooted in a monumental pot towered above their heads.

"Those are the most colossal goldfish I've ever seen," said Jurgen. He observed the tank a while. "Eight of them. I'm surprised there's room for them all."

A particularly robust goldfish with red eyes glided past the front of the aquarium. He looked at Henry in a friendly way. "I saw one at the Academy of Natural Sciences in Philadelphia almost that big," said Henry. "But it was made of fiberglass."

The gargantuan red-eyed goldfish came back around. "That was quick," said Jurgen. "I think I'll name him 'Lightning.'"

"Hello," said a little white-haired man who materialized out of the gloom behind them. He was about as wide as he was tall. The man carried two menus. "Sorry to keep you waiting. Would you like a table?"

Pim Pom, Henry, and Jurgen all looked at each other. The bottom line was, they didn't have much time to waste. They needed to find out what Tiffany Glint had been doing here on the morning of the newspaper photograph; they needed to get the M-P fueled up; and they needed to continue their pursuit of Lulu, who was most likely headed for the Orpheum, wherever that was.

Henry shook his head, since they were just there for gas. "Nobe gank woo," he said, suddenly feeling faint. He wasn't sure, but he thought he saw a pink elephant seated at the bar enjoying a cocktail.

"Weeb gorda go," said Jurgen, feeling woozy. The elephant he saw was puce and had a martini in front of it.

"Arrrrooooo," wailed Pim Pom. It wasn't clear from that outburst *what* kind of delusions might've been going through his small but capable brain.

And then, overcome by hunger and exhaustion, Henry, Jurgen, and Pim Pom fainted dead away on the floor.

When he came to, Henry was sitting beside Jurgen and Pim Pom in a dark corner of the restaurant. Jurgen fed Pim Pom oyster crackers.

"Henry," said Jurgen. "I think you passed out from hunger." He popped a few oyster crackers into his mouth. "I'm not feeling too good myself."

"I guess we should have dinner," Henry said. "We need to keep our strength up, and that half a jar of peanut butter didn't go nearly as far as I thought it would."

"Ruff!" said Pim Pom. He hadn't gotten any.

"May I take your order?" said the short white-haired man.

"Well," said Henry, glancing over the menu. "We're kind of in a hurry. Actually, we need to go as soon as we can, and we need to find a place to gas up our scooter, and maybe buy a couple— Do you know if anybody around here sells Royal Marine Rocket Flares? And we've got a couple questions for you about a customer you may have served."

"Gas, I can help you with," said the white-haired man. "Your machine will be serviced, fueled, and standing at attention when you've finished your meal. Rocket Flares—well, I'll see what I can rustle up in the fireworks shed. In the meantime, you can't travel on an empty stomach, can you?" The man had a point. Henry and Jurgen checked out their menus. There was only one entrée listed. Captain Carl's Catch of the Day. It came with iced tea and salad.

"I'll have Captain Carl's Catch of the Day," said Henry.

"Me, too," said Jurgen.

"Two Captain Carl's Catches of the Day," said the white-haired man.

"Arf!" said Pim Pom.

"Three Captain Carl's Catches," the man said, correcting himself.

"Wow!" said Jurgen, reading the description. "'Fresh seagoing creatures caught daily in the sea and served fresh to you, today, from the sea.'"

"Indeed," agreed the white-haired man, "that's right." He headed for the aquarium. Then he caught himself, turned around, and headed for the kitchen.

"Are you Captain Carl?" asked Henry as the white-haired man passed by again.

"Well," said Captain Carl, "yes." And he disappeared

into the back before Henry could ask about Tiffany Glint or Lulu.

"Say, Henry, can you spot me a few bucks?" whispered Jurgen. "I'm kind of short on cash."

"How short?" whispered Henry. "Because I was going to borrow a couple dollars from you."

"Well, I'm *completely* short," said Jurgen. "I've got nothing. Zilch. Nada. Zero. A goose egg—"

"OK, Jurgen," whispered Henry as Captain Carl approached the table with their iced teas and salads. "I get it."

"Actually, I've got eight dollars stashed in my shoe for emergencies," whispered Jurgen. "But don't tell anybody."

So of course Henry should've just admitted to Captain Carl right there that he and Jurgen were broke, and maybe they could've worked something out like washing dishes or cleaning the fish tank to pay their check, but suddenly, hunger overpowered his ability to think straight and he dug right into his iceberg lettuce before Captain Carl had even set the plates down. So did Jurgen.

"Whoa, there!" said Captain Carl, snatching his hands back. "Nearly lost a finger!"

"Sorry," said Henry.

"Sorry," said Jurgen.

"I guess we're just a little hungry," they said.

"Woof!" said Pim Pom.

"Be right back with *your* salad, sir," said Captain Carl to Pim Pom.

"May we ask you a question first?" said Henry.

"Suit yourself," said Captain Carl.

"Was there a woman in here recently, a woman named Tiffany Glint?" he said.

A funny look came over Captain Carl.

"She probably talked a lot, and was orange, and had high hair?" said Henry.

"Kind of a loudmouth?" said Jurgen.

"I'd have said more like a blowhard," said Captain Carl, narrowing his eyes, "but yes. The description does ring a bell."

"Well, can you tell us anything about her visit?" said Henry. "Anything out of the ordinary?"

"She didn't linger here," replied Captain Carl curtly. "She visited across the highway."

"At BE   ART?" asked Henry, studying the sign on the other side of the road.

"Yes," said Captain Carl.

"What does BE   ART even mean?" asked Henry.

"Perhaps while I prepare your meal you should cross Highway 99999 and find out," suggested Captain Carl.

"BE   ART," read Jurgen, gazing up at the sign.

"Sounds cosmic," said Henry.

"BEER MART," read Jurgen, looking closer and reading all the letters, including the ones you couldn't see from a distance because they weren't lit up.

"So do you think Tiffany was over here buying beer?" wondered Henry. He opened the front door. "I was sort of hoping this would be some kind of art museum."

"It is!" said the man standing in the middle of the subtly lit room amid the paintings and the sculptures.

"Captain Carl?" asked Jurgen. "How'd you get here?"

"I dug a tunnel under the highway a while back to speed my crossover," said Captain Carl. "By the way, on this side, I'm known as Curator Carl."

"Who's making our Catch of the Day?" asked Jurgen.

"I am," said Curator Carl. "Those things are actually just microwave meals left over from airline food service carts that I zap for about four minutes and charge people twelve ninety-five for. I'll knock a few bucks off your check, since you asked."

"Thanks," said Jurgen. "And actually, I'm glad to hear

they're leftover airline meals, because I was afraid you were frying your own goldfish."

"Absolutely never!" declared Curator Carl, scratching Pim Pom expertly between the ears. Pim Pom wagged every bit of tail he had. Which was of course pretty close to zero. Result: much wiggling. All of which added up to a very good character reference on behalf of Curator Carl, in Henry's opinion.

"This," said Jurgen, taking in a photo of ghostly blue lights hovering amid dark desert mountains, "is awesome!"

And even though the sight of Curator Carl scratching Pim Pom was awfully nice to behold, and he was glad Jurgen liked the photos, Henry said, "We're kind of in a hurry—"

"Right. You have some questions about my museum and its recent visitors. Here we go: The desert is a mystical place," began Curator Carl. "A place to which my humble little gallery, housed in a former Esso station, is devoted. Look around you. See the art. Read the literary excerpts displayed on the wall. Listen to the audio exhibits. Enjoy the inspiration of artists and philosophers who have explored desert places with their imaginations, like Georgia O'Keeffe, Stephen Crane, Frederic Remington,

Lennon and McCartney, Robert Frost, and Moses."

"Moses who?" asked Jurgen.

"The one with no last name," said Curator Carl.

"Oh," said Jurgen. "Him."

"I want visitors to my museum to *feel* art," said Curator Carl. "I want them to *be* art. In the desert, inspiration and existence become the same thing."

"You're losing me, Curator," warned Jurgen.

"In the pure air, perfect light, and miraculous calm of the desert, the imagination can become real," Curator Carl began again. "Ideas grow overwhelmingly powerful, yet perfectly clear. The desert is like a stage on which the dancer and audience experience the same motion, or a canvas on which the artist and the observer plunge into the scene together, or the page on which the writer and the reader lose themselves in the same story, or even the moment when you and your friend occupy the same daydream—"

"—or when a miraculous pyramid transports you into the imagination of a very tall girl?" asked Jurgen.

"Well, that's not in my official museum guide speech, but it sounds plausible," was Curator Carl's verdict. "Something that extraordinary would literally have to take place in the forty-seventh, forty-eighth, and forty-ninth dimensions, for they are the actual location where the imaginary becomes real. Although I have to say, I do get my share of scoffers, those who say the forty-seventh, forty-eighth, and forty-ninth dimensions are unattainable. In fact, there was a horrible scoffer here just yesterday morning."

"Don't tell me," said Henry. "The lady we were asking about? Big hair? Skin like a football?"

"I won't tell you," said Curator Carl. "Yes."

"Tiffany Glint," muttered Jurgen.

"Tiffany Glint," mused Curator Carl. "Well. First, Tiffany Glint scoffed at the name of my museum. 'BE   ART,' she said. 'What is that supposed to mean?' So I told her what it means—embody your dreams, embrace your visions, inhabit your imagination!"

"That must've gone over really well," said Henry.

"Like an eighteen-wheeler full of bricks," said Curator Carl. "In fact, she told me that my kind of foolishness is the foolishness that irks her most. BEER MART, she said she could get behind. But BE   ART? Pah!"

"Sounds like Tiffany," said Henry.

"But then, in the course of my duties as curator, I recounted the story of Lucius Throckmorton, which is part of the official tour. Just as she was skulking out the door, it caught this odious woman's interest, and her attitude changed," reflected Curator Carl.

"Why was she interested in Lucius Throckmorton?" wondered Henry. "And by the way, who is Lucius Throckmorton?"

"How about if I tell you the story of Lucius, and you tell me why she was interested in him?" proposed Curator Carl.

"Deal," said Jurgen.

"Lucius Throckmorton," began Curator Carl, indicating a grainy, ghostly, silver-lit photograph depicting a man in a tuxedo and cowboy boots standing in front of a black mountain range, holding a guitar and smiling a rueful smile, "sometimes known as the Singing Cowboy, was one of the most beloved country music artists in the history of Texas. His hits include 'Barbwire Kingdom,' 'Dusty Dandy,' 'Comin' Up Roses,' and 'Darkling Ghost Riders,' which plays through this speaker here every fifteen minutes."

"Hey!" cried Henry. "'Comin' Up Roses'! That's the one I heard with Lulu!"

"Really," said Curator Carl, eyeing Henry curiously. "Because no recording of it exists, and Lucius Throckmorton has not been seen since 1950."

"I heard it on the radio . . . ," said Henry. "On an old-fashioned set. At the Giant Tire Emporium. With Lulu."

"Then you are very blessed," said Curator Carl, staring at Henry evenly. "Because I have curated the art of many people in my humble museum. Painters, sculptors, musicians, performance artists, even dancers. And in my opinion, Lucius Throckmorton, the Singing Cowboy, is the most heartbreaking of them all."

"What happened to him?" asked Jurgen.

"He had an extraordinary talent," said Curator Carl, "a stellar musical imagination, and then it collapsed."

"What does that mean?" cried Henry. "We need to know what that means!" Pim Pom pressed against his leg. He picked Pim up and stroked his head.

"Ordinarily, when your imagination collapses, it means you change from somebody who could've made the world a better place into a bully, a moper, a whiner, or a jealous, resentful jerk," said Curator Carl. "A loser, a loss, a liability, a waste of breath. Sort of like that Tiffany Glint, in my humble opinion. But legend has it, this is not the fate that befell Lucius when his poor, overburdened imagination gave out."

"What happened to Lucius?" asked Henry.

"He disappeared," said Curator Carl.

"How?" asked Henry.

"Lucius Throckmorton was a simple country boy. People say he was a very sweet kid. Voice like an angel. But fame and fortune came upon him fast, maybe faster than he was ready for. After a string of hits, 'Comin' Up Roses' unexpectedly shot to number one for Lucius and his band, the Caterwaulers, in the spring of 1950," explained Curator Carl. "Lickety-split, Lucius found himself nominated for Singer of the Year. And then, just when the Caterwaulers were set to achieve true stardom, the night before Lucius was supposed to accept the award, he performed one last time at his favorite theater in Texas. During that appearance, his guitar picking became uncertain. His voice became unsure. This had begun happening in his performances, but that night it was worse than anybody could remember. Lucius stopped in the middle of a song. He gazed over the audience with tired eyes. He appeared frightened. He said, 'I'm sorry, folks. I can't imagine why I ever wanted to do this.' And then, according to eyewitness accounts, the stage lights went out, and when they came back on, he was gone. Lucius Throckmorton is never heard of anymore, except that some people say his songs still exist, in the form of ghostly transmissions trapped between the many dimensions of space and time, coming and going eternally among the hidden corners of the universe, audible to certain fortunate folks with the right kind of radio, when atmospheric conditions are perfect."

"Where did he end up?" asked Henry. "I mean, Lucius himself? He didn't really disappear! People can't just vanish. . . ."

"Old-timers in these parts say his spirit still takes the stage in the dead of night, at 3:01 a.m., on certain moonless evenings, in years divisible by thirteen, at the Orpheum Theater. It's named for Orpheus, the ancient Greek musician who once played his music in the underworld, and was never really the same after that."

"The Orpheum Theater?" cried Henry.

"Yes," said Curator Carl.

"Where is it?" Henry asked.

"In a deserted town, a ghost town, the one people always talk about but never visit: Nowhere, Texas," said the curator.

"I knew it!" cried Henry.

"And you told Tiffany all this?" demanded Jurgen.

"Well, she asked," replied Curator Carl, "and I *am* the curator."

"What did Tiffany say?" wondered Henry.

"Something odd," said Curator Carl. "Something

along the lines of, 'I was just gonna run the girl over to the ballet contest in El Paso and embarrass the cottage cheese out of her, but this is taking it to a whole new level.' I surmised that Lulu was the young woman waiting in the HumZee."

"Right, Curator Carl," said Jurgen. "She was."

"At that point in her visit," remembered Curator Carl, growing animated, "Tiffany Glint stood right there where you're standing and took a picture of this painting. When there are clearly marked signs that say no photographs."

Henry, Jurgen, and Pim Pom had a look at the painting Curator Carl was pointing at. It depicted a shadowy road, lost in gloom, leading between ghostly mountains, a road with no clear beginning and no clear end. "The Road to Nowhere," Jurgen read from the plaque beside it.

"And you're sure the Orpheum is in Nowhere?" asked Henry.

"Yes," said Curator Carl. "Nowhere, Texas, which has been a ghost town since 1963."

"And this year, right now, that we're in, is divisible by thirteen?" asked Jurgen.

"Yes," said Curator Carl. "One hundred fifty-five, no remainder."

"Did Tiffany by any chance ask for directions?"

asked Henry. "To Nowhere?"

"She made me draw her a map," said Curator Carl.

"So Tiffany has Lulu, a map to the place where, according to legend, Lucius Throckmorton once took the stage and subsequently disappeared forever, and a grudge," concluded Henry.

"Not to mention a HumZee full of gas," added Jurgen.

The Scheme of Things

"...Nowhere," said General G. G. P. Hedgerow to Phil Cicada. "Right-o. You'd like to get to Nowhere."

"Yes! Immediately!" said Phil to the general, whom he'd found dangling by the elbows of his jacket from the door of his garage in his frantic search of the house, the yard, and the neighborhood. "Good gravy, what happened to you, anyway?" asked Phil, yanking the meat cleaver, hatchet, carving knife, and World War II bayonet out of the splintery wood. General Hedgerow collapsed in a heap and then stood up and dusted himself off. To restore circulation, he performed one hundred side-straddle hops.

"Are you all right?" asked Phil.

"It's nothing," groaned General Hedgerow as the

blood began to flow back to his fingers and toes.

"In the note he left behind," said Phil, "my son, Henry, said he was headed to Nowhere looking for someone named Lulu."

"A chap must watch himself in Nowhere, you know," said the general thoughtfully, "for there one sits around and plans an endless amount of nothing for nobody, and one can squander years without realizing that one was actually supposed to be somewhere doing something for somebody."

"I see," said Phil. "I think."

"Now, let me ask you," continued General Hedgerow briskly. "Has that son of yours perpetrated this sort of caper before? By the way, mind if we pop into my kitchen for a drink of water? I've been dangling from that blasted door for over eighteen hours."

"No, he's never pulled anything *quite* like this," replied Phil, once they were in the general's kitchen, which appeared to be stacked floor to ceiling with combat rations stored in small steel boxes. "I mean, he always used to be outrageous, audacious, sometimes disputatious, but he never disappeared before."

"And his mother?" asked the general. "How is she taking all this?"

"She died last year," replied Phil.

"Very sorry, my good man," murmured General Hedgerow, taking Phil's shoulder in a surprisingly kind grip. "I believe it is now my duty to inform you," barked the general, stopping short and coming to attention, "that your Henry and his two little friends, one a small dog and the other a small boy, helped themselves to my old motor scooter. I just hope they haven't busted it to flinders by now, God bless 'em."

"I've gotta call the state police," said Phil, "and have them issue an all-points bulletin. What does your motor scooter look like?"

"I suppose its most distinctive feature," said General Hedgerow, "would be the large shimmering pyramid affixed to the side."

Phil had already bolted off to call the police. But when he realized what General Hedgerow had said, he stopped and came back. "The *what* was affixed to the side?" he asked.

"The large shimmering pyramid," said General Hedgerow. "Could've sworn it winked at me. Haven't seen such behavior since my heyday. I worked for the Queen of England, you know, became something of an expert on these matters, namely, the first, second, and third dimensions and the forty-seventh, forty-eighth, and forty-ninth dimensions, where the imaginary becomes real. Even had a nifty little prototype dodecahedron whipped up by our scientists. It was made of a classified material that, under certain conditions, would transport a trained monkey from the actual to the imaginary, so they told me, though what a monkey imagines, I haven't the foggiest idea. I also studied the many dimensions in between, which are mentioned in the work of my good friends John Lennon, rest his soul, and Paul McCartney, who once sang about a fellow who lives among them."

The general crooned, quite nicely:

"He's a real Nowhere Man
Sitting in his nowhere land
Making all his nowhere plans for nobody."

"Are you saying Henry is a Nowhere Man?" asked Phil.

"No. Not at all," replied the general. "At least not yet. But he may soon find himself mixed up with one. And I believe he may have to pass through Nowhere to get where he belongs. As a matter of fact, I believe you might have to do the same, my good fellow," added General Hedgerow, studying Phil's long, sad face.

"I just want Henry to be himself again," said Phil. "And I guess I'd like to be myself again, too."

"That's a step in the right direction," roared the general enthusiastically. "A step in the bloody right direction!"

"Where is Nowhere?" asked Phil.

"One of them is in Texas," replied General Hedgerow.

"One of them?" repeated Phil.

"There are several speculative descriptions of the coordinates of Nowhere," explained the general. "For instance, 'headed for Nowhere,' 'traveling to Nowhere,' 'ain't going Nowhere,' and, as the maestro Neil Young once put it, 'Everybody Knows This Is Nowhere.' Also, scattered across the earth's geography and all through history we find locales such as Limbo, Purgatory, the Wasteland, No-Man's Land, the Great Wide Open, the Distance on the Look of Death, A Certain Stillness Sunday Afternoons, Neither Out Far Nor In Deep—"

"Where's the nearest one?" Phil managed to wedge in.

"Texas," answered General Hedgerow. "Specific location classified, Nowhere, Texas, is hidden at the bottom of a nondescript gulch in the Crowfeather Mountains, a blank spot on the map that every living creature avoids: people, animals, plants. Many nonliving things avoid it, too: rivers, railroads, highways."

"Why does Nowhere even have a name?" asked Phil.

"Because the forty-nine dimensions all intersect there every thirteen years," replied the general.

"Where?" pressed Phil.

"Nowhere," said the general.

"Can you please not do that?" asked Phil. "This is serious."

"I'm serious, too," replied the general. "It also may be worth noting that Nowhere is a ghost town."

"Why'd it turn into a ghost town?" asked Phil.

"The usual reason," replied the general. "All the living souls gave up and left. Nowhere is a sad place, a dry and dusty place, a place like a shiver down your spine on a Sunday afternoon."

"And Henry is on his way there?" asked Phil.

"Yes, I believe that is where his search will lead him," replied General Hedgerow.

"How do you know so much about Nowhere?" asked Phil.

"Superb question," responded General Hedgerow. "You see, when I was a young man, I served in a special branch of the British military, answering directly to the Queen of England. In the summer of 1950, she assigned my unit a challenging task: to find a great Englishman who had gone missing."

"Who?" asked Phil.

"Winston Churchill," said General Hedgerow. "By the way, I mentioned all this to your son."

"What did he say?" asked Phil.

"He expressed interest," said the general.

"I see," said Phil. "The Queen asked you to look for Winston Churchill in West Texas?"

"Yes," said the general. "For you see, the Winston Churchill living in London after the war was a mere shell of the man who had led England to victory in the greatest conflict she had ever faced. His imagination, wit, and bravery were gone. We thought perhaps he was Nowhere."

"Was he?" asked Phil.

"No," said the general. "We looked all over the world and finally found him in a bar on Piccadilly. But after the other agents returned to London for good, I stayed out here to keep an eye on Nowhere, Texas. Just in case. Not the sort of place the Queen wanted to, you know, leave unattended."

"Did you figure out any more about Nowhere?" asked Phil.

"Nowhere, Texas, possesses a peculiar property," allowed the general.

"By peculiar, do you mean good or bad?" asked Phil.

"Didn't I just say," replied the general, "that Nowhere occupies a unique spot in time and space where all forty-nine dimensions periodically intersect?"

"If you could make things a little clearer?" requested Phil.

"Yes. Here is the deal with Nowhere, as you Americans say: Ordinarily, when one's imagination is in insurmountable distress, it collapses, forever exiling one from dimensions forty-seven, forty-eight, and forty-nine, where the imaginary becomes real, condemning one to a lifetime of resentment, unmet potential, and foul behavior. But if, by chance, as American musical history teaches us, one's imagination should collapse on the stage of the Orpheum Theater in Nowhere, Texas, during a year divisible by thirteen, on a moonless night, the light of one's imagination survives, preserved as a cold, blue spark that drifts endlessly among the dimensions. Through the years, faltering artists, poets, philosophers, and other brilliant types have considered this transaction a blessing, a haven. One's spark stays alive, even if it is diminished. But it's also a curse. You see, one becomes something of a ghost in the process. This is not a choice for the faint of heart."

"You have to be in the theater for this to happen?" asked Phil.

"Why, yes," said General Hedgerow. "Like I said. It's a choice. Ever since a young country singer discovered this phenomenon, discouraged geniuses have been taking the stage every thirteen years to audition."

"To be a cold blue spark?" asked Phil.

"To be a ghost light," replied the general.

"Henry is going to turn into a ghost light?" asked Phil.

"I suspect his friend Lulu is in the most immediate danger of experiencing this fate," said the general, "though Henry could be in a spot of peril, too, for it's possible that just being in the audience at the Orpheum at the proper time could trigger the transformation from promising yet dejected soul into ghost light. Yes, I'm a bit worried now. Perhaps I should've gone. But it's never wise to meddle in these things."

"I have to get to Nowhere right away!" cried Phil.

"Yes—you are Henry's father," said the general. "I believe you could justifiably butt in without seeming meddlesome. But before you go, may I just ask where Henry's pyramid came from? Simply to satisfy my curiosity."

"My wife, Melissa," said Phil. "She was a scientist. She created Elktonium. That pyramid was one of the last things she built with it."

"Then she loved you very much," said the general.

"She did," said Phil. "It's true. But how did you know?"

"Because when she left you that Elktonium pyramid," said the general, "she left you a path to follow."

"Follow where?" asked Phil.

"Back to your rightful place in the Scheme of Things," said the general. "You see, according to a favorite theory of my boss's, there are universes inside universes, and galaxies inside galaxies, and, in the other direction, going outward, getting larger, there are galaxies outside of galaxies and universes outside of universes, and this progression goes on for a long way in both directions, growing tinier on one hand and larger on the other hand, until there is no more room, and it all starts over."

"I saw those!" exclaimed Phil. "In the structure of Elktonium! By the way—your boss is really the Queen of England?"

"Yes," said the general. "Now, back to my point. In the way I just described, the dimensions run from one, two, and three, all the way up to forty-seven, forty-eight, and forty-nine. And according to the Theory of the Scheme of Things, which most brilliant scientists subscribe to, all the galaxies and universes nest inside one another like Russian matryoshka dolls, from infinitely small to infinitely large, and they know about each other. They keep tabs on each other. They watch out for each other. And once in a while, when things get dodgy in a certain location, a few of the dimensions might lend a hand to a few of the others. For instance, in our world, what if some of us lose track of where we are in the Scheme of Things, like you and your son have done? Well, if we had the right machine, say, a miraculous pyramid made of the newest metal known to man, we could get it to scan the Scheme of Things with its powerful eyeball and find out where we're supposed to be."

"So Melissa left Elktonium to show us where to go?" asked Phil.

"Yes," said the general. "Even though she herself could not have known exactly where her experiment would lead, I'd bet pounds to pup tents that your dear departed wife hoped when her son emerged from his sadness far enough to adopt a dog, which she felt he was bound to do sooner or later because of his large heart and warm soul, her equally good-hearted husband would respond by converting her pyramid into a doghouse and setting it in the backyard so sunlight would eventually hit it at just the right angle and it could begin its work."

After a brief pause to process all this, Phil shouted, "I need to find Henry RIGHT AWAY!"

"Then the Windemere-Tingley Jet Backpack, which happens to hang in my garage, might be just the thing for you," said the general.

Inside the doghouse, outside BE ART, Jurgen held a match to the fuse of Captain/Curator Carl's Fourth of July Skyrocket. Packed neatly in one corner were three Catches of the Day in to-go boxes. The M-P was pointed in a direction precisely calibrated to match Captain/Curator Carl's directions to Nowhere. If Jurgen, Pim Pom, and Henry had had more time, maybe they'd have held off lighting the rocket and used the .9 horsepower gasoline motor to drive slowly and carefully to their destination. But they didn't have more time. They had to hurry. And for people in a hurry, rockets are the way to go.

The rocket ignited. FWOOOOOOOOOM.

"Something's wrong!" Henry cried immediately from the driver's seat. "It's too powerful! I can't steer! Put it out! Put it out!" Jurgen and Pim Pom tried like crazy to extinguish the firework. But they couldn't. It was a rocket.

Burn was what it did, and once it was lit, it had to blaze until it was done.

"We've got to throw it overboard," cried Jurgen to Pim Pom. Mustering all his strength, Jurgen grabbed the tip of the rocket and, with agonizing slowness, pulled it out of the front corner of the pyramid. In his teeth, Pim Pom grabbed one of the rocket's fins and helped.

Outside, Henry did his best to keep the M-P under control. He was on the road. He was off the road. He went straight. He went in circles. He went several hundred miles an hour. He headed for a mountain. He headed for a gulch. He headed straight into the desert. After a while, he completely lost track.

Inside the Elktonium pyramid, with a heroic heave, Pim Pom and Jurgen flung the Fourth of July Skyrocket out the door. Once it was free, it flew straight for the stars, illuminating the desert, the air, and the sky above, where the sun had begun to set on their long day in the desert.

Then Henry, busy watching the heavens when he should've been watching where he was going, crashed the M-P into a road sign. He flew through the air and landed in the smelly but springy limbs of a giant creosote bush. The scooter came to a halt against a prickly pear, its transmission, along with several spokes, the headlight, the speedometer, and the horn button strewn behind it some-where in the darkness. Henry checked himself for damage and, finding none, hurried over to Pim Pom's doghouse, which had come to rest against a large boulder.

"You OK in there?" Henry shouted to the occupants of the pyramid. Battered but intact, Pim Pom and Jurgen emerged into the moonlight.

"Wow," said Jurgen, stretching the kinks out of his tailbone. "Yes. Sort of. Uh-huh."

"Eeeeeh," whined Pim Pom.

"Sorry," said Henry. "I guess the Fourth of July Sky-rocket was a mistake."

"What are we going to do?" asked Jurgen, gazing around at the collection of glittering motor scooter parts they'd scattered across the desert. He picked up Pim Pom and held him close in the evening chill.

"Put the M-P back together and get to Nowhere as fast as we can," said Henry, retrieving a handle grip from beneath a bush.

And by the light of the inconceivably distant stars above, they got to work.

"What's Tiffany Glint's angle," pondered Jurgen, locating a spoke, "with Nowhere, and the Orpheum?"

"Good question," said Henry, gathering loose nuts

and bolts. "Let's see. First, she was taking Lulu to a dance competition in El Paso to humiliate her."

"But then, on the road, Tiffany heard about the Orpheum from Curator Carl," continued Jurgen. "And she asked him a lot of questions about it."

"And she heard how a guy suffered the collapse of his imagination on the stage and disappeared forever," added Henry.

"And she sounded really interested in this story," said Jurgen. "So I'm guessing—"

"She has the same fate planned for Lulu," concluded Henry, continuing to stack parts of the old M-P in his arms like firewood. "Which means we'd better to get to the Orpheum as soon as possible, or sooner."

"But we're lost, Henry," pointed out Jurgen.

"No," disagreed Henry, after taking a pause to stare at the stars. "We're all here. That's what my mom said once, when she was an artist. In the Teleological Telephone Booth. 'We're all here.'"

"What does that mean?" asked Jurgen.

"It means," murmured Henry, "we're *not* lost."

And with that, Henry got to work arranging chrome-plated scooter parts on the ground to see if he could figure out where they were supposed to go.

Two blue stars fell slowly from the sky, the second following the tail of the first, and although Henry didn't see them because he was busy with the critically injured Muckeridge-Pressley, Jurgen did, arcing across the hem of the night and gliding toward a nearby mountain range to disappear through a gap between the peaks. Once they were gone, Jurgen saw something glittering on the ground in the starlight. Shimmering a faint green. A chunk of Elktonium. A pyramid-shaped corner of the pyramid, broken off in the crash. Jurgen put it in his pocket for safekeeping, but didn't say anything to Henry, who was occupied with the scooter and hardly needed more things to worry about, like the dinged-up pyramid.

Henry whanged away like a madman on the front wheel, which was bent. Now that Henry was hitting it with a rock, it seemed to be taking shape again.

"Henry, I have to ask something," said Jurgen.

"What?" replied Henry.

"How come you drove across half of Texas to find Lulu, but you don't even want me in your backyard?" replied Jurgen.

Henry stopped work to think this over. "Because you're real," he replied. "And you live in the real world."

"Thanks," said Jurgen. "That clears it up."

"But Lulu—doesn't really seem real," added Henry.

"And now," said Jurgen, "things are *crystal* clear."

"Jurgen, I don't feel like *I'm* real anymore," continued Henry. "I don't feel like I can do any of the things I did before—before my mom died."

"Oh," said Jurgen. "I'm really sorry, Henry. I wondered where she was when I came over. I thought maybe your parents had just gotten a divorce."

"That's OK, Jurgen," said Henry. "Thanks for saying you're sorry. And thanks for trying to make friends. But I've been on a quest to be plain plain, and not stick out, and not be who I was before. Making friends with you wouldn't exactly have been taking the *plain* road, if you know what I mean."

"Yep," muttered Jurgen. "I know. Of course, zapping in and out of Lulu's brain isn't exactly the average American pastime, Henry."

"Good point," admitted Henry. "Still, look at everything we've done together. And think about what we're about to do: find Lulu and help her get home. I sort of think we *are* friends. Because if we weren't, how could we have accomplished all this?"

"I don't know," replied Jurgen. "I guess we couldn't have. But Henry, I think we still have a few yards to go before we put this one in the friendzone."

"I know what you're doing," said Henry, smiling. "You're talking football, like a Texan. While still talking like Jurgen."

"Bingo!" said Jurgen.

That was when Henry hit the bent front wheel of the old M-P one time too many with his rock and broke three of the spokes, sending it lopsided as a rugby ball. "No!" cried Henry. "No, no, no, no, NO!" He collapsed next to Jurgen and his dog in the middle of the desert, which smelled of flowers and crossties. A breeze, warmed by the rocks that still held the sun's heat, blew across his face. Henry, Jurgen, and Pim Pom looked around themselves at the mosaic of the desert floor, an infinite puzzle of pebbles and stones stretching as far as they could see. From the spaces between the puzzle pieces, millions of tiny flower buds sprouted, awakened by the day's rainstorm.

"We came this far," he cried at the sky, "just to fail?"

The constellations and the planets stretched above him and beyond them in the moonless night, and Henry felt himself flowing out into it, among the worlds and worlds and worlds of possibility. "No," he said. "I'm not giving up. We're all here. Somewhere. And I'm going to find out where."

Henry borrowed Pim Pom's collar and used it to truss up the broken spokes.

Meanwhile, Jurgen noticed that the crash had knocked open a little panel on top of the Eagelsburger Triple-Amplified Crystal Set. On a hunch, he dug the pyramid corner out of his pocket, reached inside, and stuck it into an empty socket. Evidently, this was just what the Eaglesburger Triple-Amplified had been waiting for, because sound began to emanate from it. Henry stood slowly, listening. Music began to swell. The Eaglesburger's reception improved. In an unearthly voice, keening, high, and regretful, a man began to sing:

> *"Everything's comin' up roses!*
> *I'm the luckiest guy since Moses!*
> *Everything's coming up roses!*
> *Even when it ain't."*

His voice quavered eerily, like radio singers sometimes do on lonely nights. It had a spooky edge. Like the singer had had to swim through the dark from whatever city was transmitting his song. Like he'd started to realize that after all his struggle, drowning alone in the cold wasn't out of the question. Like he wanted to believe what he was singing, but he just didn't quite. And Henry heard, in the song, in the gloom, an entirely new meaning. Not only was it really happy; it was also really sad.

Henry dug the Speculoculars out and peered through them, wondering what it would be like to meet the singer. Evidently, they had recovered from their nasty fall on the pavement, because they started showing him what he could only believe were speculative things. At first, all Henry saw was a clear blue light hovering nearby, two or three feet off the ground, drifting gently away from him, but slowly the light resolved into the shape of a man, a man walking sadly through dark shadows. Henry recognized him from his photograph: Lucius Throckmorton, the Singing Cowboy, as he must've looked on the day he recorded the song. The Singing Cowboy was thin; his Adam's apple bobbed up and down in his throat like a kernel of loneliness he could never quite swallow, and his eyes were as deep as oceans. Lucius turned, looked straight at Henry, beckoned him to follow, and disappeared along an old dirt road snaking between two desert mountains.

"Everything's coming up roses," sang Henry softly. "Even when it ain't."

"That's the road to Nowhere," observed Jurgen. "Just like in the painting."

Yippee Ki Yi Yay!

"I thought this was supposed to be a ghost town," said Henry as he, Jurgen, and Pim Pom pushed the wobbly old M-P into an alley. Lucius Throckmorton, who hadn't looked at them again after he waved them along the road to Nowhere, slipped through the stage door of the Orpheum. "But look! People are lined up around the block to get in."

"We'd better buy tickets," said Jurgen. "It must be getting close to showtime. I still have eight bucks. Curator Carl didn't charge us after all, when it came to light that the Catch of the Day comes from surplus airline carts."

"I hope they allow pets," said Henry. Pim Pom bounded ahead.

But the box office was closed when they got to it, and the line in front of the theater had dwindled to nothing.

Nobody was tearing tickets at the front door, anyway. So they slipped into the Orpheum.

The only empty seats were in the front row. They crept up the aisle and sat.

"What's going on?" wondered Henry, scanning the crowd. "Are we in the right place? Is this where Tiffany brought Lulu?"

"Look," said Jurgen, pointing to the music on the conductor's stand in the orchestra pit.

"The *Firebird Suite*," whispered Henry. He turned to a little old lady sitting across the aisle. "Is there a ballet recital today?" he asked.

"Not so much a recital as an audition, young fella," said the little old lady, eyeing him closely. But Henry hardly heard her answer, because, even in the dim light of the theater, he could clearly see the *E* of the Exit sign. Right through the little old lady's left eye.

"How—what—I'm sorry—*who* are you?" stammered Henry, gazing around only to realize that he could see through everybody else in the audience, too.

"Well," said the little old lady, "we're the citizens of Nowhere. Lucius was the first of us, and ever since he disappeared right here back in 1950, we've been coming, a few at a time, every thirteen years, to do just what he did.

Take the stage, say good-bye to anything and everything we ever imagined, and vanish bluely into the night. By the way, I'm Thelma Klaus. I won the Rampart Prize for poetry in 1978, before I ran out of things to say."

"But you didn't disappear, Thelma," protested Henry. "At least not all the way. You're here, even though you're see-through."

"You're right. We're all here," replied Thelma, glancing around. "And a little bit transparent, as you have been kind enough to point out. We've come to see the new people audition. Soon we'll fade away again, and for the next thirteen years, we'll be nothing but the bluest spark of what we once were, haunting empty spaces."

"You'll be the bluest what of what you once what?" asked Jurgen.

"Ghost lights," clarified Lucius Throckmorton quietly from the orchestra pit, where he'd taken his place behind the conductor's podium. "We'll go back to being ghost lights."

"And people say I can't figure stuff out," chuckled Tiffany Glint, sliding into the seat beside Henry. "Hooweeee."

Lucius raised his baton. In his tuxedo and his gleaming cowboy boots, he cut a dashing figure. He counted to four, and then, on the downbeat, the little orchestra in the pit of the Orpheum launched into the Introduction to the *Firebird Suite.*

"She's gonna flub this up something awful," chortled Tiffany Glint. "And freeze up. And fail. And go blank. And I don't know what all. And end up disappearing for good among all these spooks and specters and whatever the heck they are! Like that see-through Saran Wrap old biddy just said. And that doofy loser at the museum. Imagination collapse. Lost in the dimensions. Yeah. OK. Whatever. This is so much better than just taking her to El Paso and turning a bunch of persnickety ballet judges loose on her!" Tiffany turned her attention to the curtain. "Ya dang Olive Oyl giraffe-legged stork!" she catcalled. "Ya ridiculous knock-kneed stumblebum ostrich! Who are you kidding? Thinking you were ever gonna dance on those snowshoes a yours, on the Spirit of Raisin float, or anywhere else!"

Lucius shot an alarmed look over his shoulder as he conducted, but he didn't stop the music. He didn't seem to be able to.

"Lulu," Tiffany persisted. "You ain't gonna be dancing the role of the Firebird! You gonna be dancing the role of the Dodo Bird! Girl, people see you clomping around up there on the stage like that dang old bird that brought

Dumbo to his mama, they're gonna hightail it for the exits like a buncha Girl Scouts when a skunk shows up at the marshmallow fire!"

Thelma leaned toward Henry. "What's that strange individual next to you hollering about?" she inquired.

Henry studied Tiffany. For a few seconds, he was too appalled to move, speak, or think. He'd never seen Tiffany in person before. She was mean. She was cruel. She was as awful as he'd imagined.

"She's a bully," whispered Jurgen. "I know. I've seen my share."

"But why's she disrupting the auditions?" asked Thelma.

"'Cause I pulled a fast one, Grandma!" shot back Tiffany, her eyes bright with glee. "I tricked a little uppity twelve-year-old fancy pants into entering these here auditions for Casper the Friendly Ghost or whatever the heck ya'll think you are, and now she's gonna turn into a phantom just like you!"

"But she's too young," said Thelma. "Lucius! Stop the music! The next performer has been forced to enter against her will! She's only a child! She has her whole life ahead of her. This is a decision for grown people. She shouldn't be allowed to make it."

"That's why I made it for her," shot back Tiffany. "As her legal guardian. And now that Lulu is headed to where she belongs, maybe I can return to my rightful place in the scheme of things, getting lots of attention in the parade. As the Spirit of Raisin." The last three words dripped with more venom than the fangs of an eight-foot rattlesnake.

"Please stop, Mr. Throckmorton," pleaded Henry.

"I can't," whispered Lucius over his shoulder. "Not unless that poor girl behind the curtain wants to quit right now and give up and say good-bye and turn cold and blue and go with us. 'Cause once the music starts, the show has to go on, and if she wants to keep on being a real girl when it's finished, she's got to dance. And I mean really do it right. 'Cause if her imagination collapses up there, she'll be coming with us when the curtain drops."

"Lulu doesn't want to quit," declared Henry. "That much, I know."

"She might, boy," said Tiffany, eyeing Henry with distaste. "After all the excellent work I done done on her brain, she just might. I personally think she's ready to give up and say bye-bye. Who are you, anyway? You seem more solid than these other folks."

"I'm Henry Cicada," said Henry. "And I can't say I'm pleased to meet you."

"Wasn't expecting you to," retorted Tiffany.

Henry turned toward the stage. "We're here, Lulu!" he called.

"We came to cheer!" hollered Jurgen.

"Aroooo!" howled Pim Pom enthusiastically.

"Shut it, bug-boy," snapped Tiffany.

The curtain drew back. Lulu stood like a swan in headlights, frozen, her chin up, her shoulders back. Slowly, she began to wilt. In the spectral spotlight pouring down from the balcony, Henry saw the glitter of a tear as it slid from the corner of her eye.

Lucius threw himself into his conducting. "Come on, Caterwaulers," he called. "Let's help this little lady out of her predicament!" And they gave it all they had. Two violins, a drum, and a harmonica.

Still, Lulu didn't move.

"Figures. Pathetic old pelican," sneered Tiffany.

All the while, the audience flickered. "We were never like her," said Thelma, gazing at Lulu. She gestured at the crowd. "We were bewildered, scared, tired, old. We knew our imaginations were done, and knew we were out of ideas, and we'd soon just turn into selfish, ornery, noxious disappointments to ourselves and others. So we came here. And took the stage. And failed our auditions, and let our visions flicker out, and became small blue sparks, so we didn't have to go dim completely. We *meant* to flub our auditions. For us, to lose was to win. But that girl up on stage doesn't belong here. She needs to succeed. She needs to dance her heart out."

"Lulu," Henry called from his seat. It came out softer than a whisper. "Lulu," he called. He knew he had one chance to help her. But he had to make her hear.

Henry tried to stand up. It was harder than anything he'd ever attempted. The weight of his entire life pressed down on him, everything he'd tried to do right but done wrong, every battle he'd fought but lost, every friend he'd tried to help but hurt, everybody he'd loved and let down. He struggled. His legs trembled with the effort. Henry put his hands on the armrests and pushed. But he could not rise.

The crowd grew restless. Lucius and the Caterwaulers played on. None of them wanted Lulu to fail, like they'd done. These were sad old ghosts, but they were not mean ones. And Lulu was missing her chance. Her debut would also be her farewell. Tiffany had figured it all out and won. Henry could see. Soon, Lulu's hopes, her dreams, her imagination would be done for.

If only he could tell her one thing—if only he could

get one sentiment across—

Henry managed to get halfway to his feet, and fell back into his red velvet theater seat. The effort to stand had exhausted him.

Tiffany turned to examine Henry. "Yaaaaaah," she jeered. "Ya loser. Sit there and suffer. That's right." She glanced around at the crowd. "It seems like it'll be easy, don't it? Just stand up to your fears, they tell you. And follow your dream. And express your talent. And envision your vision. And all that crud. But it ain't easy. Believe me."

"Wait—" said Henry. "You—"

"Yeah. I used to be different," said Tiffany. "I was a artist. Ever since I was a little girl, I could twirl that baton. I could make you hold your breath in expectation, make you sit up straight on your bleacher seat, make you stand and cheer, put your heart in your throat with the magic and daring of the twirling and tossing of which I was capable."

And as Tiffany told him of her talent, Henry could hear a change in her voice. Henry realized that for once, she was telling the truth.

"I would just look up into the sky, and imagine a feat of twirling prowess, and I would *execute* it!" exclaimed

Tiffany. "I could take what was in the hearts and minds of my audience, their aspirations and their ambitions, their hopes and dreams, dad-gummit, and embody their thoughts in the silvery, glimmering twirling of my baton. I could! I did! 'Cause I was a artist!"

"What happened?" asked Henry.

"State baton twirling championships. Arlington, Texas, November 17, 1994," snarled Tiffany. "Runner-up. But I shoulda won. I was robbed. Robbed, I tell you! I only dropped my baton 'cause the sun was in my eyes. And the wind blew. I know. It was in a indoor facility, but still. And a old lady sneezed. And a baby cried. On purpose. And the whole thing was rigged! 'Cause I was the best. I could twirl my baton like falling off a log! But—but—but—after that, I just couldn't do it so well anymore. I couldn't put my heart in it. I couldn't give it my all. 'Cause that was just too durn hard. And why should I have to do something hard? So I quit trying. I mean, I could still spin the baton fast, but I never tried to put any real zip on it after that. And ever since then, I've been—"

"Mean," finished Henry. He tried to point accusingly at her, but his arm felt like lead.

"Well," said Tiffany. "If you want to put it like that. Yes."

"Neither here nor there," Henry added. He wanted to stand and confront her, but he couldn't feel his feet.

"OK, sure, whatever," Tiffany grudgingly allowed.

"Lost between the imaginary and the real," Henry persisted weakly. He meant to give her an indignant glare, but his head suddenly felt too heavy for his neck to hold up.

"Enough already," said Tiffany.

"You're the one who belongs up on that stage," whispered Henry.

"Nobody likes a know-it-all, cowpoke," grumbled Tiffany. "Besides, shut up, 'cause Lulu's goose is cooked, and your gander is fricasseed, and who cares what you think? You ask me, you ain't looking so good, boy. You ask me, you're gonna end up floating through space glowing all tiny and blue by the time this is over, just like the Pink Flamingo up there."

"Thelma? Could he?" asked Jurgen in alarm.

"There *are* certain extremely outrageous and pertinacious people," said Thelma, regarding Henry closely, "whose very *lives*, when you get right down to it, are like works of art."

"Hmmmm," said Jurgen.

Henry struggled in his chair against an invisible

weight pushing down on him.

"I don't mean works of art like sculpture, painting, music, or dance," said Thelma.

"What *do* you mean?" asked Jurgen, because the look on Henry's face said he wasn't in a good place to ask follow-up questions. "Henry? Are you OK?" wondered Jurgen.

"What I mean is, sometimes just being *around* particular folks feels like being lifted out of your own life and put down somewhere different, more interesting, and in the end, better," explained Thelma. "And that effect is their masterpiece."

Jurgen thought back to the bone and the astronauts of Kuala Lumpur. He thought back to the tactical and poetical defeats of Theotis, the pyramid, and the rocket-powered trip through the desert. Then he turned to Henry. "Different and more interesting, one hundred percent of the time." Briefly, Jurgen thought back to the stepladder from which he had dangled for a while. "Better? Ninety-five point two."

"You—really—are a good friend," Henry struggled to tell him.

"We've definitely gained enough yardage to make the friendzone," Jurgen agreed. "And we're still going." Then he looked closely at Henry. "Henry, what's wrong?"

"He seems like an audacious sort of boy," said Thelma, peering at Henry, too. "As if just being *him* takes all his imagination. And as if, at times, he can make the imaginary become real for those around him. That's his great achievement."

"Couldn't have put it better myself," said Jurgen. He saw Henry struggling to breathe. "Henry?" he cried in alarm. "Are you all right?"

"So if he fails to be himself—" began Thelma.

"If Henry isn't Henry?" clarified Jurgen.

"Yes," replied Thelma, "if Henry can't be Henry tonight, here, in this theater, right now, then I am afraid he'll meet the same fate I once did."

Henry tried one last time to stand. And fell back. And pushed upward again. And fell back.

"Henry! No! Come on!" Jurgen cried.

"I—can't," gasped Henry. "I think I'm done."

"Here, Henry, come on," said Jurgen. He gave Henry his hand. And with a mighty heave on both their parts, Henry stood.

"Hey!" said Tiffany in alarm. "Sit down!"

At that second, Henry's dad jetted through the theater doors and zipped up the aisle.

"Do you people ever give up?" wondered Tiffany as she eyed the jet pack wearily. "You keep coming at me in waves, like a little army of goobers."

Stumbling out of his backpack, Phil took in the scene. "Henry! Wow! Outrageous!" said Phil. And as he uttered the word "outrageous," Phil gave Henry the look, the look that reminded Henry how much he reminded Phil of Melissa.

Which made the weight pushing down on Henry even heavier. He dropped back into his seat with a groan.

Which made the look in his father's eyes become a little bit sad.

Which made the weight pressing on Henry even heavier.

Which made Phil's look even sadder.

Which, as they stared at each other, made Henry's sadness heavier than it had ever been. *All this time*, Henry thought to himself, *I've been landing inside Lulu's imagination while it's imploding, and I never realized mine is doing exactly the same thing.*

Tiffany rubbed her hands in glee. "Hey, look," she cackled. "Henry's brain is about to go wonky, too! Double whammy! For the win!" And she turned back to Lulu, who had crept almost near enough to the black curtains at the back of the stage to disappear from sight once and for all.

Pim Pom curled into a ball.

"Come on, Henry," urged Jurgen. "Think of something."

So Henry thought of something: "We're all here, Dad," he whispered.

"That's what your mother said," murmured his father.

"I mean," said Henry, "I'm still here, and you're still here, and *she*'s still here. Everything she knew and understood and imagined."

"Even though she's gone," said Phil.

"I still love her," said Henry.

"I do, too," said Phil.

"I'm outrageous, Dad," said Henry. "It's who I am. It's what I do. I just can't help it."

"I've been waiting to hear you say that since we moved to Texas," replied Phil.

"I can't stop being me, Dad," whispered Henry. "Or I'll disappear." And like that, the weight lifted off Henry Cicada. He saw in a blinding flash that his outrageousness was the best way, the perfect way, and maybe the *only* way to keep his mother's spirit alive. He realized that if he let it slip away, then she'd slip away, and he'd slip away, and his dad would, too, along with Lulu. And on top of that, Jurgen and Pim Pom would be pretty sad to see them go. "*I* was the one headed for Nowhere all along," he mused softly. "And now I'm here."

Henry leaped to his feet. He hopped onto the seat of his chair. At the top of his lungs, he hollered, "YEEEEEEEEEE-HAW!" just like Texas people do. Only possibly a bit louder. As soon as he let it rip, he understood why all these Texans liked yelling it so much. It felt good!

A ripple of astonishment passed through the audience. It'd never occurred to them to stand up and cheer for Lulu, even though they were pulling for her to succeed just as much as Henry was.

Lulu looked straight at Henry and she smiled.

A bit of her musical accompaniment remained. So she started dancing.

Henry didn't know much about ballet, as he was the first to admit, and Lulu obviously had a lot to learn, but he could tell she had potential. It was easy to spot.

From the orchestra came the unmistakable voice of Lucius Throckmorton. "YIPPEE KI YI YAY!" he called. And with that, he dropped his baton, picked up a guitar, and joined right in on the *Firebird Suite*.

Lulu stood tall, caught her balance, flexed her knees,

looked downright fierce, and launched into her tour jeté. Really *launched*. The crowd fell silent. After all, this was exactly the opposite of what they'd come to Nowhere to commemorate. Lulu was not Nothing. She was Something.

Lulu danced. She danced and made mistakes and needed a lot of improvement and had a long way to go, but she threw herself into it, and she wasn't afraid, and by the end, she was joyful.

In the silence after Lulu finished, Henry heard breathing. It was Lulu, panting from effort. He heard Tiffany Glint gnashing her teeth. Her heard Pim Pom's toenails in the aisle as he trotted to the edge of the stage for a better look. He felt his dad's arm around his shoulder.

And he heard Lucius Throckmorton call, "BRAVO, LITTLE LADY!"

"GO GET 'EM, COWGIRL!" hollered Jurgen.

"Hooooooooooo!" howled Pim Pom.

"For the love of Tony Romo," muttered Tiffany Glint.

And then came the applause.

And Lulu's bows.

And then, quietly, the ghostly, dimensionless inhabitants of Nowhere, Texas, filed slowly out into the lobby of the theater to evaporate into whatever dimensions and locations they were fated to inhabit when they weren't gathered together, one moonless night every thirteen years, in Nowhere. The procession took a while.

On his way past, Lucius Throckmorton, the last guy out, caught Henry's attention and winked.

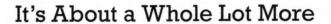

It's About a Whole Lot More

And then, slowly, all the fizz went out of the place. Henry found himself in a dark, dusty theater, weakly lit through grimy windows by glittering stars. He still sat in a red velvet theater chair between his father and Tiffany Glint. Slowly, all around, the walls of the Orpheum began to dematerialize. In the starlight, Henry saw Lulu sprinting up the aisle toward him, her tutu flouncing, her stride exultant. By the time they came face-to-face, the theater had disintegrated around them. Nothing remained but the charred timbers of its walls and a historical marker on an iron post noting that the actual Orpheum Theater had burned down in 1963. The one dusty street of Nowhere stretched into the distance. At the curb lurked Tiffany's HumZee. A dry gulley carried no water from one no-place to another. And over it all, silver-black mountains loomed in a giant, hulking ring.

"Are you OK?" Henry asked.

"I'm perfect," said Lulu. "How about you?"

"Excellent," said Henry. "Awesome performance."

"Thanks," said Lulu.

"Awwwwww," cooed Tiffany nastily. "Ain't you just a pair a little sweetie pies."

"You're still here?" Jurgen asked her. "I thought maybe you'd disappear with all the rest of the ghost people."

"Are you kidding me? I ain't got time for that cheese dip!" scoffed Tiffany.

"Maybe," whispered Jurgen to Henry, Lulu, and Pim Pom, "she never had enough imagination to qualify for Nowhere in the first place. Maybe instead of turning into a blue light that wanders among the dimensions, she just turned into a monumental jerk."

"Maybe. So what? Stranger things have happened, shrimp," retorted Tiffany. She fell silent as she rummaged around in her purse. "Now. I know we're all in a hurry to get back home to where we belong, and put this behind us, and forget about it, and go ahead with life as usual, and I agree that *would* be a fine idea."

"After all this," began Lulu, "I don't know if it'll be so

easy to go back to business as usual. . . ."

"But I got a different thought," said Tiffany. "And here it is!" From her purse, she extracted a hank of beef jerky. "Lulu, I done missed my chance to take care of you when Nowheresville or whatever it's called was up and running. And I regret that. But my regret won't keep me from taking care of you right now!"

"I think the days when you could push me around are over, Aunt Tiffany," said Lulu, shivering a bit in her tutu.

Phil draped his Windbreaker over Lulu's shoulders and stepped toward Tiffany. "Ma'am," he said, "I have to ask you to leave the children alone."

"Sir, could you give me a second?" asked Tiffany. She dug around in her giant purse some more. "Here we go," she said, extracting a contrivance of small interconnecting stainless steel rods that she expertly assembled into—

"A collapsible majorette baton?" said Phil. Henry could see him fighting down the urge to ask if she'd like one made of Elktonium.

In milliseconds, Tiffany had her baton twirling as fast as a buzz saw. Before anybody realized what she was doing, she clocked Phil under the jaw with it, knocking him cold.

"Dad!" cried Henry. "Dad!"

"Aw, he'll be fine when he wakes up," said Tiffany, tossing the baton into the car. She dangled her desiccated strip of beef jerky in front of Pim Pom. "Here, poochie! Check it out! It's a premium brand! Slim Jim! Come and get it!"

"Pim Pom!" cried Henry. "No!"

But it was too late. Pim Pom, hungry, trusting, and overwhelmed by the temptation of beef jerky, leaped into Tiffany's arms. In an eyeblink, she dropped the bait in the dirt and zipped all of Pim Pom up in her purse except his head, which she left sticking out between the sharp brass teeth of the zipper so he could breathe. Barely.

"Hnnn, hnnn, hnnn," whimpered Pim Pom, pleading with his eyes for Henry's help.

"Let him go!" demanded Henry.

"Aunt Tiffany," begged Lulu. "What are you doing?"

"Showing you who you mess with," said Tiffany, "and who you don't. You guys all like this little dog?"

"Yes," said Henry, Lulu, and Jurgen in unison.

"You wouldn't want anything to happen to him?" pressed Tiffany.

"No!" they cried.

"Well, swell!" said Tiffany. "Cause something's about to. Say good-bye to your mutt."

"He's not a mutt!" cried Henry. "Let him go!"

"Hah," scoffed Tiffany.

"Everybody—rush her!" cried Henry.

"Not so fast, Dandelion Head," sneered Tiffany, twisting a handful of Pim Pom's only remaining ear.

"Aieeeeeee!" yelped Pim Pom.

They all froze.

"One more step and I yank it clean off!" screeched Tiffany.

Tiffany eased back on Pim Pom's ear. But she didn't let go. She snaked her other arm around Pim Pom and fumbled in the bottom of her purse for her HumZee keys. Slowly, she backed toward the ludicrous car.

"What are you doing, Aunt Tiffany?" asked Lulu.

"You're real attached to this pooch, aren't you?" responded Tiffany Glint.

"He's the best dog ever!" declared Henry.

"That's *just* what I wanted to hear!" cackled Tiffany. "Tell you what. Since you *adore* him so much, I'll give you a chance to say good-bye." She opened the door and climbed into the driver's seat, never relaxing her grip on Pim Pom. "Say good-bye."

"Where are you going?" asked Henry desperately.

"Away," said Tiffany.

"But where, Aunt Tiffany?" pleaded Lulu.

"To drop your little waggy pal off on the other side of the mountains," snarled Tiffany, "where the coyotes live. He'll last, I estimate, ten minutes."

"Why?" wailed Henry.

"'Cause you *all* have to pay!" snarled Tiffany, slamming her door. "And this will just about do it!"

"I'm afraid I have to object," said Phil, regaining consciousness enough to lift himself up onto one elbow.

"Go ahead," said Tiffany, cranking up the HumZee with a roar. "Object away, Professor. Object till the longhorns come home. I'm headed over them hills in my vehicle to take this fella to the other side of Nowhere. Don't wanna be late delivering coyote snax! Hah!" Tiffany patted Pim Pom's head and put her clown vehicle in drive. "Think about *that* when I'm up on the Spirit of Raisin float and you're pushing a broom behind the horses, Lulu."

"But, Aunt Tiffany," pleaded Lulu, "I already told you. I don't want to do the parade float. It's all yours. There's no reason to be mad."

Tiffany put her machine back in park. "You think this is about the parade?" She laughed. "Honey, it's about a whole lot more than that."

"What's it about, then?" asked Henry.

"Revenge!" shrieked Tiffany. "On all you superior-acting people! With your dancing and your outrageousness and audaciousness and superiordinariness and this little tiny kid over here and the old guy dressed like a spaz and whatever else hoo-hah that you think makes you the best and brightest, well, who cares about it, because now you can just spend the rest of your lives wondering whatever became of your friendly neighborhood puppy!" She wrenched Pim Pom's ear again, viciously, just to be cruel, and tossed her purse, with him in it, into the passenger seat. "Bye-bye, losers."

With that, she gunned her ludicrous truck straight toward Henry, Jurgen, Lulu, and Phil.

They dove for the cracked old Nowhere sidewalk. As Tiffany roared past, Jurgen climbed to his knees and shouted into the driver's-side window, "Hey! I was talking to your boyfriend!"

Tiffany shot flaming rays of rage at Jurgen from her eyes as she passed. She kept her foot on the gas for a hundred more yards, spraying gravel into the emptiness of the ghost town, and then, in a cloud of dust, she locked up all four wheels of the HumZee. Henry could see Tiffany pounding her steering wheel in frustration. Then she jammed the HumZee into reverse and they had to dive aside again as she roared back toward them. "You," she said, rolling down her window by pressing one blood-colored fingernail on the button and pointing at Jurgen with another, "were talking to Austerlitz McFadden? Did they let him outta jail already?"

"Y-yes," said Jurgen, glancing at Henry. "And Austerlitz McFadden said—"

"Did Austerlitz McFadden say something about me?" demanded Tiffany. "*What* did he say about me?"

"How did he know about Austerlitz McFadden?" Lulu whispered to Henry.

"He didn't," Henry whispered back. "He used a special technique to guess."

"Cool," said Phil, shaking the cobwebs from his brain.

"Austerlitz McFadden said," began Jurgen, "that you like it when he calls you . . ."

"Tiffy Top?" cried Tiffany in horror. She put her HumZee in park.

"Uh-huh," nodded Jurgen.

Tiffany switched off her four motors and clambered down from the driver's seat to square off against Jurgen.

While she was busy doing that, Henry began creeping around the HumZee to the passenger side.

"No way!" said Tiffany. "He told you that? When I get my hands on that weasel— Hey—wait—I see what you're up to—" She caught sight of Henry, and before he could get to the door of the HumZee, she reached behind herself and snatched her purse off the seat with Pim Pom in it. Glancing around wildly, she backed up against the steel side of her machine and clawed the air in front of her like a small, outlandishly manicured grizzly bear. "Stay back, everybody! Stay back, or the poochie pays!"

"During the heyday of the Orpheum Theater," recounted Phil, reading information off a fireproof iron historical plaque in front of the building's charred foundation, which amounted to the same thing as doing research, which was of course his specialty, "luminaries such as Bob Hope, Lucille Ball, Sid Caesar, and Lou Costello performed inside its walls!"

"Quiet!" shouted Tiffany, brandishing her HumZee key like a weapon. "I know what you're trying to do. Outrage me. Upstage me. Confuse me. Bamboozle me with all your shiny, smart skills! Well, I ain't letting go of the dog!"

Lulu performed a few pliés to limber up her legs.

"There once was a lady from Raisin," began Henry.

"Hey," said Tiffany. "Hold up. I'm from Raisin. Is that

about me? You getting disputatious with *me*? 'Cause I'd a thought you'd a learned your lesson by now—"

"Whose skin tone occasioned much gazin'," Henry continued.

"Watch it, smart boy," warned Tiffany.

But Henry said:

> *"She tinted her hair*
> *A color so rare*
> *Yale scientists found it amazin'."*

"I'm. Taking. The. dog," insisted Tiffany through clenched teeth. Her hands shook. She fumbled her keys and dropped them in the dirt. Setting down her purse, she scrabbled for them in the dust. Pim Pom tried to dig his way out of the handbag. But he only had one front paw.

Phil, observing his surroundings closely, saw another old sign nailed to a tilting telephone pole beside Tiffany's HumZee. It had a big red *X* on it. "No Parking," he read.

"Stuff a sock in it," growled Tiffany.

"There once was a lady from Texas," announced Henry.

Phil and Jurgen tried to circle around either side of

Tiffany to snatch Pim Pom. She saw them, grabbed Pim by the neck with her left hand, and squeezed. Phil and Jurgen froze. "Where are my ding-blasted keys?" she cried.

"Who parked her HumZee where the X is," Henry plowed ahead.

"For your information, I didn't see the sign," retorted Tiffany. "Now! Enough!"

Still Henry pressed on:

> "When the tow truck appeared
> It was just as she feared:
> The driver was cross-eyed and reckless."

"Ain't no reckless cross-eyed driver gonna tow my baby!" objected Tiffany, stretching an arm protectively across her HumZee. "I ain't gonna stand for it! Wait. This is a ghost town. What am I talking about? Ghost towns don't have tow trucks. Why am I even listening to you? Where are my keys? How am I gonna get out of here?"

Henry, Jurgen, Lulu, and Phil all shared a glance. Their shenanigans were working. Against this outrageous volume of imaginative output, even Tiffany's pigheaded narrow-mindedness hardly stood a chance.

"Is that the sun coming up between two mountains

in the east?" whispered Henry.

"I hope so," said Jurgen, "because it's been a long night."

"I been messing around with you clowns long enough," declared Tiffany, coming up with her keys. "Adios."

And then, in the morning air, the sun popped over the horizon. It climbed quickly. Soon, it approached an angle of five and a half degrees.

And although it was dinged and dented and missing a few corners after its recent crash, Pim Pom's doghouse began to glimmer gorgeously in the alley beside the ruins of the Orpheum.

"I just hope," whispered Henry loudly, "she doesn't figure out how to use the *pyramid* to get away from here." If he could sucker Tiffany into jumping inside the pyramid while it was activated, he thought, then maybe it would take her where she needed to go, which was bound to be someplace awful, and hopefully far away.

"SHHHHHHHHHH!" said Henry, Lulu, and Phil all at once. Pim Pom redoubled his effort to dig through the bottom of Tiffany's purse. "She'll hear you."

"What? I *did* hear him," said Tiffany. "You don't want me to use the pyramid? Like get inside it? To get away? Is that how you guys have been going places?"

"Just don't!" cried Henry. "Don't get in it!"

The eyeball appeared. Carefully, it took in the scene.

"You're saying you don't want me to get in it?" asked Tiffany.

"Right," said Henry. "That's what I'm saying." Out of the corner of his eye, he watched Lulu limbering up.

"Then that means you *do* want me to get in it," said Tiffany. "'Cause you think you're so smart, and you think you can fool me into doing what you want me to do by saying the *opposite* of what you want me to do."

"Oh, heck," said Henry dejectedly. "You figured out my strategy."

"But if you *do* want me to get in it," reflected Tiffany, "then it's probably because something terrible is going to happen to me in there. So what I'm gonna do is, I'm gonna throw in the dog!"

"No!" cried Henry as the doghouse approached full power in the morning sun's rays.

Pim Pom pawed at the floor of Tiffany's monster purse like the terrier he was born to be.

Tiffany ran toward the doghouse.

Pim Pom squeezed through the hole he'd dug and leaped to the ground.

Henry scooped him up.

The Elktonium shimmered more furiously than Henry had ever seen it shimmer.

Lulu stuck out her long, limber leg.

Tiffany tumbled headfirst toward the pyramid.

Jurgen nudged it slightly so she'd plunge straight through the door, and as she did—the whole shebang disappeared.

Some People Never Learn

Turns out that, at exactly the same time Tiffany was tormenting a sweet, trusting animal, someone made a clerical error at the Hornblende Correctional Facility, on the outskirts of the town of Antler, somewhere in the wide open country of the Texas Panhandle. Inmate 3355, one Melvina Carbonara, had been allowed to go home six years early. The error was so complicated that nobody knew it had been made. No one realized that Melvina had walked right out of her cell that morning, mistakenly escorted by a guard who had received a memo from the main office reading, "Let Melvina go home after breakfast." There was an extra "m" in the memo. It was supposed to have read, "Let Melvina go *hoe* after breakfast," which would've indicated that Melvina's assignment at the correctional farm was to chop weeds with that particular tool. But the typist got in a hurry. It was nearly the end of her overnight shift.

Maybe they should've made the inmates pull up weeds with their hands at Hornblende, and avoided the potential "hoe/home" confusion altogether. For just about the time Melvina was walking through the front door of the prison, a glimmering pyramid materialized out of thin air, while nobody was looking, right smack in the middle of a special exhibition of art created by the inmates. A painting teacher from nearby Glass Mountain High School had helped them create it because she thought that everybody, even people in jail, ought to be allowed to use their imaginations once in a while.

And so Tiffany Glint emerged into yet another scenario where the imagination becomes real. Only this one also happened to be inside a prison. The eyeball seemed amused by this.

"Melvina!" barked one of the guards who, like everybody else at Hornblende, had no idea the real Melvina had just been released. "Melvina, you are not authorized to attend this exhibition. Get back to your cell!"

Tiffany, a little dazed from her Elktonium-aided flight, looked up. Why, she wondered, was this chick in a blue uniform calling her "Melvina"?

"Melvina!" said the guard. "You lose some weight? And what happened to your face? It's orange. Clashes with your jumpsuit. You better start putting on a hat while you hoe weeds, Melvina. The sun's doing funny things to you."

The guard, thinking that the pyramid was one of the exhibits, moved it out of the corner of the gallery into the light, near the refreshments table.

Of course, Tiffany raised a huge stink, claiming not to be Melvina. She claimed she didn't belong in prison. (Boy, the guards had never heard a prisoner say *that* before!) In the ensuing argument, a small riot erupted, during which the punch bowl got kicked over, sending a tidal wave of lemonade sloshing toward the edge of the refreshments table.

The eyeball at the top of the pyramid stared upward in fear, awaiting its doom, for remember, lemonade dissolves Elktonium.

And then at the last second, as the citrus inundation spilled off the table overhead, the eye seemed to spy something in the distance: flight plans, travel orders, clearance for takeoff. It flickered away into nothingness just before the lemonade soaked it, saving itself, but in the process doing away with any chance Tiffany Glint had of getting out of prison for the next six years.

Henry and His Friends Won

And so, Henry and his friends won.

"Wow," said Henry, gazing up at Lulu. "You're really tall."

"I know it," said Lulu.

Phil told Henry, "You'll be the same size as Lulu before long."

"What are you talking about, Dad?" asked Henry.

"One of these days," said Phil, "you're gonna grow into those feet of yours. And when you do, you and Lulu are gonna make quite a pair."

"They already do," observed Jurgen.

Arf! Arf!

Lulu asked, "How are we getting home?"

"That horrible orange woman left her HumZee behind," observed Phil.

"Gah," said Henry.

"I'm never riding in a HumZee again," added Lulu.

"I'd rather walk," tossed in Jurgen.

Pim Pom wee-weed on the tire. "Arf! Arf!" he said.

"I have to agree with Pim Pom," said Phil. "Hey. I've got the Windemere-Tingley Jet Backpack. But I doubt it's strong enough to lift us all."

"We could pile on the old M-P," proposed Henry. "Although it's kind of small."

At that moment, the pyramid rematerialized, safely back from Hornblende. It hummed and glowed and sat sort of crookedly with one corner on the curb so that the sun, even though it was climbing fast, still hit it at an angle of six degrees. The eye, a little bit wild after its recent brush with disaster, seemed to calm down when it caught sight of Henry waiting for it in the clear, cool dawn air of Nowhere.

"Look!" exclaimed Henry. "Pim Pom's doghouse is back. Wanna see where it takes us?"

Acknowledgments

Thanks to Marisa de los Santos, Julianna Baggott, Dave Scott, and Jennifer Carlson, who have been rooting for Henry since day one.

Thanks to Susan Janes Johnson, Catherine Dean-Gooderham, and Macon Sheppard, who contributed their wisdom, wit, and intelligence to Henry's advancement.

Thank you to the intrepid Alice Jerman, editor extraordinaire, for embarking on this escapade. Thank you to the bold Jennifer Klonsky for her hospitality, enthusiasm, and encouragement. Thank you to Andy Smith, Sarah Creech, and Alison Klapthor for making Elktonium look just like I've always imagined, only more. And thank you to Alexei Esikoff, Elizabeth Ward, and Gina Rizzo for being so eager to explore all forty-nine heretofore unknown dimensions!

Thank you to the readers of Cedar Lane Elementary for their spectacular ideas.

Finally, thanks to Viki Lynn Teague, for reading all those books out loud.

31901056955190